Alexander

Harlowe Savage

Copyright ©2022 by Harlowe Savage

All rights reserved.

No portion of this book may be reproduced in any form without written permission from the publisher or author, except as permitted by U.S. copyright law.

Thank you so much to everyone who supported me through this process! You mean more to me than I can express.

Harlowe

Chapter One

Alexander knew what was expected of him. His father, Phillip II of Macedon, had no shortage of women. Growing up, Alexander had known at least seven women who had been introduced to him as his father's new wife over the course of his life, and that wasn't counting the dozens of courtesans that frequented the King's bedroom on a rotation. When he was still too young to understand what was going on, his mother, or one of their many servants, would shoo him off to bed before the ladies came filtering in. As he entered his formative years, however, the servants couldn't keep him in one place for any given period of time and as his bedtime grew later and later, so did his late night escapades around the palace. He would often see the ladies going in and out of his father's quarters, so by the time he began his schooling, he had an archive of questions to ask.

"Aristotle," Alexander looked up from the texts he was supposed to be studying.

"Yes, Alexander," his teacher responded, not glancing up from his own reading.

2 ALEXANDER

"Why do so many ladies come to the palace at night?" Aristotle choked on the wine that he had been drinking and took a moment to collect himself. Of all the questions he'd expected Alexander to ask, this certainly was not one of them.

"Well," Aristotle began, scratching his beard. "They come to see your father. You know that your father is a very powerful man, and well... women find that... attractive."

"So they just come to see him? At night? That sounds like a terrible time to visit a person." Alexander scrunched his nose and Aristotle looked desperately from servant to servant in question. For gods' sake, had nobody had "the talk" with him yet? The instructor took a deep breath and ran a hand through his hair.

"Alright. I suppose we are having this conversation now." Aristotle walked over to where Alexander was sitting and plopped down onto the bench next to the boy. "You know that you have a mother and a father," he began, and Alexander nodded. So far so good, Aristotle thought.

"They made you through a process called intercourse. It is a functional, yet enjoyable, activity that can be used to make children." Aristotle paused, glancing down at Alexander to make sure he was following. "The women that your father is married to, including your mother, have... um... intercourse with him, for the reason of creating children, like yourself."

"Okay." Alexander nodded slowly. "So is Father trying to make children with the ladies who visit him at night too?"

"Well," Aristotle continued, "no, not exactly. You are your father's heir, but any children that came to be from the ladies that visit him at night would not be, so they would have no purpose. One day, you will have a wife and produce an heir of your own. The women who visit your father do not have that purpose. Intercourse can be an activity exclusively for making children, but it can also be an activity that adults participate in for enjoyment, and... that is why those women visit your father at night. For enjoyment... Do you understand?"

Alexander pursed his lips and leaned back on the bench. "I guess. Is this something that all adults do?"

Aristotle sighed and shrugged. "Most adults, yes."

Alexander scrunched his nose in disgust. "Do I have to?"

Aristotle took another gulp of his wine. "To produce an heir, yes. But outside of that, no, I suppose not."

Alexander never pushed his instructor on the subject again after that, but he did sneak out of his room that very night secretly following one of the ladies to his father's chambers to see for himself why anyone would want to participate in such activities firsthand. He hid in the curtains just outside the room and peeked through gaps in the fabric, watching curiously as the women dropped their robes. Alexander frowned, their breasts were round and their nipples stood erect in the chilly air. He watched as his father kissed each woman on the lips and down their necks, appreciating and lovingly caressing each curve. He listened as they moaned and panted like animals in heat and as his father mounted one of them from behind, Alexander decided that he'd seen enough. When they were all distracted, Alexander slipped away unseen and went to bed, puzzling over what everyone could possibly think was so great about intercourse.

Years later, Alexander was made regent of Macedon at 16, while his father was off conquering Byzantium. His mother threw him a huge party in honor of his newly appointed regency and he'd actually been having a great time until his mother called him into a back room to introduce him to a woman named Callixena. She was several years older than him and sported a very curvy figure, with curly brown hair that cascaded around her waist.

Objectively, she was very attractive; her large brown eyes reminded him of his mother's and she looked very similar to some of the women that Alexander had seen entering and exiting his father's chambers over the years, he wasn't so far removed that he couldn't acknowledge that much. When his mother left them alone, Callixena had pressed her breasts up against him and brushed her hand over his cock suggestively.

To her confusion, however, Alexander was not amused and asked her to leave immediately. When she told him that his mother had requested she seduce him, Alexander shook his head in disappointment and gave her a couple of tetradrachms to leave him alone, retreating to his chambers. He was prepared to spend the rest of the night alone, sulking in his room, but his best friend had other plans. Together, they spent the evening out on the balcony laughing about his mother's plot and drinking wine Hephaestion had swiped from the party.

He knew how extremely lucky he was to have a friend like Hephaestion. Hephaestion had never judged him for being who he was and had remained by his side, despite the pressure placed upon him and consequently those around him as he trained to take his father's place one day. Alexander trusted him inherently and knew that Hephaestion would be by his side until the day he died.

Alexander woke to the sound of his double doors opening and the servants shuffling in. He stretched and squinted as Thetima threw open the curtains letting in the morning sun. His silk sheets shifted over his tanned body; the years of training had built his muscles, giving him a toned silhouette that progressively grew slimmer tapering in from his broad shoulders.

"Thetima…" Alexander groaned, rubbing his eyes with the heels of his palms. "Why are you waking me so early? I thought court didn't convene until later today."

Alexander flipped over and hugged a pillow to his chest so that his chin was positioned on the pillow, glancing sleepily at his favorite servant. Thetima was an older woman in her forties, though Alexander frequently told her she didn't look a day over thirty; she had taken care of him since he was a child and, despite the fact that he was an adult now, she never let him forget it.

"I have a letter from your father." After throwing open the curtains, Thetima turned away from the balcony and moved towards Alexander. In her right hand, she held a piece of parchment, dirty and clearly worn from travel. "He requests your presence on the front lines."

Alexander sat up immediately, accepting the robe handed to him. Suddenly, he felt much more awake.

"The Athenians have convinced the Thebans to join them in their opposition of your father and his army. So, the king would like you to lead a cavalry unit out to his position and offer support."

Alexander stood, his robe draped around him, and took the letter to read for himself. It was, in fact, his father's handwriting and while it was a far cry from an admission of need, the gist of it was still the same.

CHAPTER ONE

"Understood." Alexander nodded, allowing the servants to remove his robe, and begin to replace it with his riding armor. "Has Hephaestion..?"

"He is in the stables readying your horses," Thetima replied, straightening his shoulder pads. "We woke him first, immediately when the letter came in, so he could gather the cavalry and have everything prepared for you when you came down."

Alexander couldn't help but smile, the corners of his mouth upturning ever so slightly. Of course, Hephaestion was already preparing for the journey. As if there had ever been a question of who was going to accompany Alexander to the front lines. He took great solace in the fact that if Hephaestion was prepping everything, he didn't need to worry; everything would be ready just the way he needed it by the time he got there.

"Excellent." As the servants completed the finishing touches on Alexander's armor, he handed the letter back to Thetima. "Shall we?"

Thetima nodded, gesturing for the servants to open the doors and Alexander strode out of his room with the confidence of someone twice his age, the confidence that could only be explained by years of study and training to become the ultimate war machine. Alexander had been studying battle tactics since he was five, using them in the games he would play in the courtyard with Hephaestion and the servants to ensure victory, returning to the drawing board when something didn't work out the way he'd hoped. He was fluent in three languages by the time he was seven, excelled at swordsmanship and archery by nine, and had read the entirety of Aristotle's literary stock by fourteen.

For his fifteenth birthday, his teacher had given him his personal, annotated copy of the Iliad and Alexander had taken it with him on every venture outside the palace since. Reading calmed him, stilled his mind, and helped him prepare for whatever lay ahead, so when he grabbed his satchel from the side table on the way to the stables, he didn't need to check to know that the book was there.

Walking out the huge double doors of the palace, Alexander scanned his gaze across the courtyard until it fell upon a flash of black hair dashing out of the stables and over from the group exiting the palace grounds. Alexander grinned as his friend ran directly to him, tossing an arm around his shoulders.

"There he is!" Hephaestion grinned and squeezed Alexander tightly. "I have the horses ready and the rest of the cavalry is lining up just outside the city gates. As soon as we arrive, they will be ready to ride."

"Ah, Hephaestion," Alexander quipped, wrapping his arm around the dark-haired man in return. "What would I ever do without you?"

"Die, probably," Hephaestion chuckled, dodging Alexander's playful lunge at the comment. "But don't worry, you'll never have to find out."

Alexander blew air out of his nose in a laugh. "Oh good; you had me worried there for a second."

Hephaestion threw his head back and laughed, shoulders shaking. It was a comforting sound, Alexander mused. He figured that he could probably be happy for the rest of his life just riding into battle with his best friend and hearing that laugh. Alexander reached out for his horse and mounted it easily.

"Come. My father is waiting for us."

"Ah yes, can't let him face the big, bad Thebans all by his lonesome, now can we?" Alexander laughed and brought his horse to a trot, Hephaestion matching his speed to his right.

"I suppose not."

Alexander began heading towards the city gates, steering his horse as needed. Every now and then, however, he found himself glancing to his right. Not to make sure that Hephaestion was still there, he knew he would be, but rather just to look at him. Hephaestion continued to grow long after Alexander had stopped and much to his chagrin, stood half a head taller than the prince. Despite Hephaestion telling Alexander how much he envied his sunny, blonde hair, Alexander always thought that Hephaestion's wavy black hair and dark eyes were far better. Objectively, Hephaestion was stunning and only getting more so with age.

They rode hard through the day and only began to slow as the sun started to set, not wanting to tire the horses before battle. Alexander declared, as the sun dipped below the horizon, that they would build camp and rest there for the night.

"Fuck. It's been such a long time since I rode an entire day through." Hephaestion sat heavily in the chair in Alexander's tent and kicked his feet up. Alexander trailed in after him and slumped onto the bed, knocking his shoes off and tucking his legs up underneath him. "What I wouldn't give for a good blow job right now to get my mind off my aching ass."

Alexander rolled his eyes and pulled out his well-loved copy of the Iliad. This was not a first, Hephaestion would sometimes talk about things that were outside of Alexander's typical comfort zone, usually just glossing over the details when he didn't respond. This time, however, Alexander wasn't so lucky.

"What about you?"

"What about me?" Alexander responded curtly.

"A blowj... come on Alexander, stop acting like you've never gotten a blowjob before." Hephaestion tilted his head to the side, adjusting himself in his armor and leaning back.

"I haven't," Alexander said bluntly, turning the page in his book.

CHAPTER ONE

"You..." Hephaestion for once seemed to be at a loss for words. "Alexander, you are the heir to the throne; surely you have women throwing themselves at you left and right."

"I do," Alexander sighed, finally lowering the book into his lap and looking up at his friend. "Doesn't mean I'm interested."

Hephaestion blinked in disbelief, opening and closing his mouth a couple of times before finally landing on keeping it shut. "Well, you have to get tired of fucking your fist, don't you?"

"What are you talking about?" Alexander saw several emotions flash across his friend's face at once.

"Gods Alexander, what do you do when you get hard?" Alexander furrowed his brow and shook his head, putting his book down next to him.

"I just wait for it to go away; what the fuck are you supposed to do?" Alexander snapped, losing his patience. Hephaestion considered Alexander for a moment as if he was trying to decide exactly what he was supposed to say. Slowly he sat forward, fingers pressed to his lips.

"You can... touch yourself," Hephaestion began slowly. "You... well... you wrap your hand around it and..." Hephaestion touched his fingertips together and began moving his hand up and down. Alexander blinked a couple of times in confusion and pursed his lips together, trying to decide what he was thinking about asking. "It feels really good," Hephaestion finished, sitting back into his chair and rubbing the back of his neck awkwardly. "I just..."

Hephaestion stood up and shrugged, making his way to the door. "Try it sometime." He grinned and hurriedly took his leave of the tent, leaving Alexander alone with his thoughts.

Fucking his fist?

Alexander shook his head and began taking off his armor and clothing to get ready for bed. Absolutely ridiculous. He had gone 18 years without resorting to such things, he didn't need to try it out now. He'd made the decision years ago that he wasn't interested in that sort of thing. If he didn't want to do it with other people, why would he want to do it alone?

Try it sometime.

Alexander blushed remembering Hephaestion's words. Did that mean that it was something Hephaestion did often?

It feels really good.

Alexander felt his cock begin to fill as he laid down. 'Traitor,' he thought, reluctantly throwing a dirty look downwards. Alexander took the book from the foot of his bed and set it on the bag next to him. Placing his hands behind his head, he stared up at the roof of his tent and focused on willing away the heat gathering in his belly. Unfortunately, unlike the times when this had happened to him before, his cock didn't seem even remotely interested in letting him wait it out.

You wrap your hand around it and...

His cock twitched in interest. Scowling, he glanced down at his crotch. The blankets over him were tented up, mocking him. Sighing, he weighted his options. He could try to go to sleep?

Unlikely.

If he waited until it went down on its own, he'd likely get less sleep than he intended and he liked being well rested going into battle.

But...

If he accepted Hephaestion's advice to just "take care of it"... Rubbing his eyes in defeat, he reached over and extinguished his lantern, leaving him in complete darkness. Somehow, the darkness of the night made him feel less self-conscious about what he was going to do.

Closing his eyes, he let his hand snake down his chest and under the covers. Almost as if his cock knew what was about to happen, it twitched again and produced a bead of liquid at the tip. For what seemed like an eternity, Alexander rested his hand on his hip, contemplating every decision he had ever made leading up to this moment. Then finally, he inched his hand over the length and gently wrapped his fingers around the shaft. The moment he gripped himself, his hips jerked slightly, moving his hand and sending a wave of pleasure through him.

Oh.

Experimentally, Alexander gripped a little tighter and gave himself an exploratory stroke. When he did, a noise escaped his lips that he'd never heard himself make before, somewhere between a yelp and a sigh. He stopped dead still and tensely listened to the noises around him, suddenly hyper-aware of his surroundings. Fires crackled and some of his soldiers laughed jovially with each other, clinking their cups together, but he didn't hear anyone calling his name or walking in his direction. So, he bit his lip and stroked himself again.

More prepared this time, he kept his lips shut and closed his eyes.

Oh, fuck.

As he moved his hand, he felt a warmth beginning to build in his lower abdomen. He wasn't sure exactly what was going on, but it felt better and better with each stroke, so he didn't stop. His heart rate began increasing like he was in battle and he felt his breath coming out in stuttered puffs. Quickly, before more whimpers escaped from his lips, he brought his free hand up to his mouth and bit down on his knuckles.

He felt his cock leaking and as he continued to massage the length, his palm became lubed with the precum dribbling from the tip. He felt dangerously close to something. What that was, he wasn't sure, but he couldn't bring himself to stop. Images of Hephaestion describing this to him flashed through his mind and for some reason, that caused the coil wrapped tightly within him to snap. He arched his back as the muscles in his whole body pulled tight, intense waves of pleasure like he'd never experienced before shot through him, making his legs shake and his toes curl.

Once it was over, Alexander collapsed back onto the bed, boneless and breathing heavily. Somewhere in the back of his mind, he registered the sticky feeling on his hand and cock, but did nothing about it. He fell asleep, never having felt quite so calm and rested in his entire life.

2

CHAPTER TWO

Alexander made his way out of his tent and across the field to his horse, Bucephalas, patting her gently on the nose in greeting. He'd been careful to wipe clean his sheets and body of the sticky, white fluid that he'd fallen asleep in the night before, prior to leaving his tent. Evidently, this was something that many people did and the last thing he needed was someone recognizing what had transpired in that tent the night before and bringing it up.

He pet Bucephalas a few more times and reached into his bag for a carrot he kept for her. He wasn't sure why he was so embarrassed about everything, but part of it probably had to do with the fact that he had pictured his friend's face as he reached his climax. Despite being assured that this was a common practice among men his age, he was pretty sure *that* part was not so normal.

But even now, in the daylight, as he recounted the pleasure he had felt, his cock twitched in interest and he sighed. Sure, it had taken care of the problem in the moment, but instead of making

CHAPTER TWO   17

things better, he found himself wanting to do it again. It was as if indulging this one time had opened the floodgates. Hephaestion had been right. It had felt really good, incredible even, but he couldn't afford to be distracted riding into battle. So, he pushed it down, back into the depths of his mind, promising himself that he'd think about it more upon returning to the palace and hoping that would be enough.

The rest of the ride to his father's camp was fairly uneventful. Aside from joking and bantering with Hephaestion every now and then, they rode mostly in silence. Hephaestion hadn't brought up the conversation they'd had last night and Alexander was grateful. Frankly, he wasn't quire sure what he would say. As they rode, Alexander could not stop thinking about how he'd reached his peak to images of his friend and he really needed time to figure out how *he* felt about it before talking about it with someone else.

As they rode over the final hill, they finally caught sight of the camp. The sun was beginning to set again and the remnants of the last fight were trickling off the battlefield, back to their respective sides for the night. Alexander truly did love being a military man and he always swelled with pride whenever his father called for him in his time of need or trusted him with an important task back home.

Two years ago, his father had been leading a front in the war against the Thracians to the North, when he declared Alexander as regent. During that time, there had been some discontent from a few of the local tribes causing trouble. Alexander had swiftly managed that, driving them from their territory and naming the land Alexandroupolis out of sheer spite. When his father had returned, he praised his son for his military prowess and sent him out with a small team to wrap things up. Of course, he had dealt with it swiftly and masterfully, returning to his father a conquering hero.

Alexander hopped off Bucephalas and handed the reins over to a foot soldier. His father was waiting for him among the generals in his army. Grinning, he clapped Alexander on the back.

"Excellent. Now that Alexander was here, we will finish this deftly and promptly." The generals nodded in welcome as he was herded into the generals' tent. He could feel Hephaestion on his heels and allowed his lips to turn up slightly as he sat down. He didn't even need to ask anymore; Hephaestion knew that his place was right at Alexander's side. He fought the urge to turn over his shoulder and grin at the man. Now was not the time to be getting distracted; he needed to turn his full attention to the plan his father was laying out for him.

"Alexander will come around the back and handle the left, flanking them." Philip pointed to the board with his riding crop. "I will command the right and as we move up this hill, we will bottleneck them and cut off their reinforcements."

Alexander nodded dutifully, but if truth were to be told, he was incredibly distracted. He could sense Hephaestion's presence with every fiber of his being. The closeness pulled his consciousness in two directions, one behind him and the other desperately attempting to pay attention to the strategy meeting.

Once the meeting concluded, Alexander exited the tent and turned to head back in the direction where his own was being set up. He paused as he felt a hand wrap around his wrist. Hephaestion pulled Alexander into a nearby tent and looked around briefly to ensure that they were alone.

"You okay, man?" Hephaestion asked, placing a hand on Alexander's forehead.

Alexander wanted to answer, he really did, but for some reason, the proximity was causing his mouth to dry up. He could feel the edge of the tent on his back and Hephaestion's hand on his head, burning into his skin. His friend looked at him, his black hair hanging slightly in front of his eyes. Alexander blinked a couple of times and pursed his lips in an attempt to regain control of his faculties, but all it actually did was give him the opportunity to lock eyes with Hephaestion.

He'd never really taken the time to look before. Well... he'd looked, but he'd never really looked into Hephaestion's eyes. Sure they were dark, but they were also littered with golden flecks that caught the light each time his gaze shifted. His eyes flicked down to Hephaestion's mouth for a moment and he found himself wondering what those lips would taste like. He'd never been interested in kissing anyone before. In fact, the idea of kissing any of the women that his mother had tried to set him up with actively repulsed him, but for some reason, he couldn't help but wonder.

The sound of a soldier shouting brought him back from his daze and he laughed, batting Hephaestion's hand away. "Yeah, I'm fine," he quipped. "It's just been a long two days of riding and I'm ready to lie down."

Gracefully, he maneuvered under Hephaestion's other arm and backed up to the opening of the tent. He smiled at his friend and rubbed the back of his neck. "Shall we head back?"

Alexander kicked himself internally for letting himself get caught so horribly off guard and for a second, he thought that Hephaestion was going to call him on it. He watched several emotions flash across his friend's face before he finally landed on a teasing grin.

"Yeah, let's do that." Alexander let out a breath he didn't know he had been holding and turned, walking out of the tent. Again, he felt his friend following him, until the presence migrated to his side. They walked back together to their side of camp in a comfortable silence that they had practices for the many years they'd been friends. Alexander turned and gave Hephaestion's shoulder a pat before heading into his tent, intending to go over the plans his father had given him. Just because he was having some sort of crisis didn't mean that people weren't depending upon him for the battle tomorrow. His men's lives literally rested in his hands; he needed to get it together.

CHAPTER TWO

The morning came far too soon. Alexander had finished going over the plans at a decent hour, but little did he know that his problems had only begun when he laid down to go to sleep. Without the dam intact to hold in his thoughts, the second his mind wasn't on something else, he felt his cock harden under the covers. He had to actively avoid touching himself anywhere below the waist because, just when he would begin drifting off to sleep, his hand would brush his thigh and his dick would stand up again. Was this just going to be his life now? Getting hard all the time until he gave in and took care of it?

Sure, he could have just dealt with it, but it was the principle of the thing. He hadn't forgotten how he'd felt in the tent when Hephaestion had cornered him and frankly, he was worried that memory would make its way into his head while he was... dealing with his problem. So, he suffered in silence. It took him three times as long to fall asleep, but at least he didn't have to deal with the additional guilt of starting something knowing where his mind would take him.

As Alexander sat on his horse at the front lines, looking down into the shallow valley of enemies, he clenched his jaw and breathed mindfully to keep himself present. As soon as his father gave the signal, he would sweep down the side and launch his flanking attack. Alexander kept his eyes trained on his father and his father's generals, waiting for the exact moment... when...

There.

Philip turned his horse around and signaled a retreat. Just like they'd planned, the army turned tail and began retreating back towards camp, and just as they knew they would, the enemy followed. Alexander held his hand up to ready the riders and waited patiently until a majority of the enemies were past his entry point.

"Now!" Alexander shouted, thrusting his fist forward in the air. He kicked Bucephalas in the side and leaned forward, charging down the hill towards the enemy. Behind him, he could hear the shouts of his men and the pounding of the horses' hooves on the ground. A couple of the enemy soldiers turned their horses around seeing his army's approach, but it was far too late. The majority of the Thebans were committed to following the retreat and, as Alexander charged in, his father's army turned back around, blocking any escape.

Alexander drew his sword and swung, catching a few Thebans in his wake and carnage ensued. It was a brutal fight, but at the end of the day, as soon as the Thebans had followed Philip's retreat, the battle had been decided. Once the remaining enemy soldiers had been collected, Alexander turned Bucephalas around and rode back to the camp. He was sore, as one would be after being hit repeatedly by swords and spears, even through armor, but he'd certainly been through worse.

Unfortunately, his body seemed to disagree with his assessment, and as he hopped down off of Bucephalas, he felt his knees buckle underneath him.

"Alexander!" He heard Hephaestion's voice as his knees hit the ground. Instinctively, his hand went to his torso, and when he felt a sharp pain in his side, he pulled his hand away seeing that it was now bloody. "You're bleeding."

Hephaestion knelt down beside him and hoisted Alexander's arm around his shoulders, standing up and providing balance for the both of them. "You got stabbed and then kept fighting, didn't you?" Alexander shrugged noncommittally, feeling a little light-headed. "You asshole. You lost a lot of blood. Come on, let's get you patched up."

Alexander allowed himself to be led back into his tent and placed onto the bed. Hephaestion began the typical routine that they had whenever one of them got hurt. First, he pulled off all of Alexander's armor, and his shirt for good measure. Then, he got a bowl full of water and used a rag to begin cleaning up the gash.

It wasn't life-threatening, but he had lost a lot of blood, so he could do very little other than lie there as Hephaestion cleaned him up. He hissed reflexively when he felt the first stitch go in, closing his eyes to focus on his breathing.

"Yeah, I know," Hephaestion murmured between stitches. "There. Sit up."

Alexander took Hephaestion's extended hand and sat up slowly. After ensuring that Alexander wasn't going to pass out from sitting up, Hephaestion grabbed the bandages he'd set to the side and began wrapping up Alexander's torso.

"You really should be more careful with yourself," Hephaestion scolded, clicking his tongue on his teeth.

"I know." Alexander shrugged. The room was beginning to stabilize, so he covered one of Hephaestion's hands with his own, trapping it between his hand and bandaged torso. "Thanks."

When Hephaestion didn't respond, Alexander looked up and found himself in a very familiar situation. Once again, Hephaestion was very close to his face - from leaning in to bandage him - and he found himself locking eyes with the dark-haired man yet again. Alexander parted his lips to say something, but as soon as he did, he suddenly found that he couldn't remember what he was about to say.

Was it hot in here? Or was it just the blood loss?

Wait... No... blood loss made you cold.

Hephaestion looked back and forth between Alexander's eyes, and he could have been hallucinating due to the blood loss, but Alexander swore that he looked down at his lips like

Hephaestion had done the night before in the tent. Hephaestion took his free hand and slid it up Alexander's arm, softly gripping his bicep, and despite himself, Alexander found himself leaning forward slightly into his touch.

He always took such good care of him... and he was so pretty... gods, Alexander really wanted to kiss him.

Their noses touched and Alexander realized how close they had gotten. All he had to do was lean in a couple of centimeters more and their lips would be touching.

It would be so easy...

He was so close...

So...

"Commander."

The pair jumped apart at the sudden voice at the tent entrance. Alexander averted his gaze and cleared his throat. "Yes."

At his acknowledgment, the tent flaps were pulled open and one of his father's guards, Pausinias, walked in. "Ah, I see you were injured." Alexander had known Pausinias since he was a child and for some reason, having him walk in on what felt like an incredibly intimate moment made it so much worse.

"Oh... um... not too badly. Hephaestion just stitched me up." Alexander turned his full attention to Pausinias, only far too aware of how Hephaestion moved to pick up the spare supplies and stand to leave. "Can I help you?"

"Yes. I was told to come get you for announcements. I will tell your father that you will be out momentarily." Hephaestion had made his way to the door and nodded at the general.

"Sir."

"Hephaestion." The general nodded back. "Please, if you wouldn't mind, I need some assistance rounding up the troops."

"Of course, sir." Hephaestion smiled at the general and snuck a quick apologetic glance to Alexander. Who of course waved it off and smiled back sheepishly.

As the tent flaps closed, Alexander found himself alone with his thoughts yet again, he felt his face heat up and buried it in his hands.

What the fuck was that?

3

CHAPTER THREE

They didn't speak of it on the ride back. In fact, they hardly spoke at all. As far back as Alexander could remember, he could not think of a time when things had been this uncomfortable between the two of them.

It was all his fault.

He'd ruined things by being weird after Hephaestion had teased him for never touching himself. Alexander had gone and thought about Hephaestion and then couldn't bear to be in the same space as him without blushing with shame. He wasn't exactly sure what had happened in the tent when Hephaestion had patched him up, but he had been loopy due to the blood loss and probably did something that made Hephaestion feel uncomfortable.

Fuck.

As they rode back into the city, Alexander lost sight of Hephaestion entirely. Expecting him to be waiting just outside the stables, Alexander stepped out into the brisk night air and looked around. However, aside from a few guards meandering around, he didn't see anyone. Ducking his head back into the stables, he checked the stall next to where Hephaestion boarded his horse.

Empty.

Alexander sighed, feeling his stomach clench. Was Hephaestion avoiding him? Gods... he'd never forgive himself if he fucked up this friendship. Alexander ran a hand through his hair and drifted slowly back to his room. Every time he would turn a corner, he would lift his gaze from the floor and look around. He told himself he wasn't looking for Hephaestion, but each time he looked around and didn't see him, his chest tightened a little more.

Finally, he kicked open his bedroom doors, wandered over to his bed, and sulked. He started slightly when he heard a noise behind him. Whipping around, eyes wide, he gasped in surprise.

"What are you... Wait. Hephaestion?" Alexander dropped the bag he was holding and stood, blinking in disbelief. Hephaestion looked sheepish, not quite meeting his eyes. Several times he opened his mouth like he was going to say something, only to shut it again and rub the back of his neck as he was wont to do when he was uncomfortable.

"I was looking for you-"

"I'm really sorry, Alex-"

"What?" they asked simultaneously, after speaking over one another.

"You were looking for me?" Hephaestion asked, expression confused and slightly guilty.

"What could you possibly have to be sorry about?" Alexander shot back.

Hephaestion pursed his lips and furrowed his brows, the way he did when he was thinking really hard about something. Timidly, Hephaestion stepped around the bed and leaned against the dresser at the end.

"I..." he started.

"You've been avoiding me," Alexander mumbled, feeling that tightness in his chest again.

"No!" Hephaestion replied, a little too loudly, flushing and leaning back, both his palms flat against the dresser. "I... Yes. But it's not what you think."

Alexander lifted an eyebrow and Hephaestion cocked his head slightly to the side. "To be fair... I don't know what you think, exactly... but, um..."

Alexander waited patiently for Hephaestion to get his thoughts together. Neither of them were particularly good at talking about emotions, or anything vaguely deep. Over the years, they had developed a routine of noticing when the other was out of sorts: bringing them wine or pastries, sitting out on Alexander's patio, and looking at the stars until they felt better. But for some reason, this didn't feel like it was something that could be swept under the rug with pastries and fine wines.

Hephaestion visibly swallowed and looked up at the corner of the room. "I'm sorry. I teased you about not ever... um... I know you're uncomfortable with anything vaguely sex-related. You've been acting strangely with me since then; I crossed a line and I'm sorry," Hephaestion finished in a huff, peeking over at Alexander through his hair.

Alexander put his hands together to speak, but stopped, holding up one finger. "You think you made *me* uncomfortable?" Alexander asked incredulously, grinning slightly at the absurdity of it all. He took a breath to keep talking but made the mistake of looking up and meeting Hephaestion's gaze. His words caught in his throat. Hephaestion was staring at him with wide eyes, unmoving from the position he had been in before. "I... mean..." Alexander attempted sloppily, trying to salvage the situation from backsliding into an area where he would need to explain himself, but it was too late.

"I didn't?" Hephaestion asked softly.

CHAPTER THREE 31

"Um..." Alexander was now the one looking sheepishly around the room. "No, you didn't."

Hephaestion pushed off from the dresser and put a hand up, eyes squinting slightly. "You always hated it when I talked to you about girls in the palace, and when the other soldiers started fucking the chambermaids, you looked like you were about to pass out as they told stories around the fire."

Alexander nodded weakly. His brain was moving a mile a minute, but unfortunately for him, none of that brainpower seemed to be going towards formulating an excuse that would get him out of this conversation.

"The way you were looking at me, Alexander." Hephaestion took a tentative step towards him, dropping his hand back down to his side. "I've never seen you look at me like that. I thought I must have seriously fucked up for you to get so uncomfortable and embarrassed."

"You, um..." Alexander shrugged, resigning to his fate, and simply told the truth, "gave me some things to think about."

Hephaestion was still staring at him and keeping his distance, like he thought that Alexander might slap him across the face or yell, "Just kidding!" at any moment. He licked his lips slightly and let his eyes dance between Alexander's, searching for answers.

"You're looking at me like that right now."

"Yeah." Alexander couldn't even deny it. He felt nailed to the floor where he was standing and, for the life of him, could not stop looking at Hephaestion's lips.

"You tried it?" Alexander flushed deeply at the question, answering wordlessly. Hephaestion took a deep breath and looked around as if trying to solve a complicated problem. "But you were always disgusted whenever anyone spoke about sex and never even considered any of the girls that your mother threw at you."

Alexander huffed in frustration. "Well, I didn't realize that I had any other options before." The second that the words passed his lips, his eyes grew to the size of saucers and he froze. From where he was looking, he couldn't see Hephaestion approaching him, but he could hear it. The soft padding of his shoes on the marble floor, coming closer and closer. His heart began to race.

Suddenly, he felt a hand on his jawline, bringing his face up to meet Hephaestion's gaze. Alexander was certain that Hephaestion could hear his heartbeat; it was so violent and unrelenting that there was no way he hadn't noticed it. Experimentally, Hephaestion leaned in slightly before stopping, their lips inches apart.

"Tell me to stop." Hephaestion whispered. He almost sounded frightened, like he was terrified he was misreading the situation catastrophically.

CHAPTER THREE

"I don't... want to," Alexander managed between breaths.

He heard Hephaestion's breath hitch and then he was leaning in again, his other hand landing on Alexander's waist and pulling him in slowly. When their lips touched, Alexander could feel Hephaestion shaking. He didn't have any idea what he was doing, but he hated when his friend was upset, so he pushed his chin forward incrementally, pressing his lips back against Hephaestion's.

Hephaestion adjusted his hand so that it cupped Alexander's face and deepened the kiss. Not expecting it, Alexander was not prepared for the noise that came out of him, very reminiscent of his night alone in the tent. The second the moan made its way past Alexander's lips, all caution got thrown to the wind. Hephaestion stepped forward, pushing Alexander up against the closed door, his arm pulling him in closer and closer, their hips flush.

He licked at Alexander's lips and instinctively, Alexander opened them, allowing him access. His tongue was hot and tasted like wine; everywhere he touched scorched Alexander to the bone and left a tingling sensation in its wake once the hand was gone. As if possessed, Alexander flung his arms around Hephaestion's neck, pulling him in even closer. He ran his fingers through Hephaestion's beautiful black hair and allowed his tongue to explore the other man's mouth.

Hephaestion's hands wandered, sliding over Alexander's sides and grabbing at his hips. When Hephaestion moved his palms from Alexander's hips to his ass, Alexander nearly melted. He gasped, pressing his hips forward and unintentionally grinding his hardening cock on Hephaestion. He would have felt horribly embarrassed if it hadn't been for Hephaestion's equally aroused length pressing back into him. Instead, all he felt was pure, unbridled lust like he'd never felt before.

Hephaestion's hips rocked up against his, his breath in Alexander's ear, and his hands gripping his ass as if his life depended on it and suddenly, Alexander understood. Things began clicking and falling into place one by one, every story he'd ever heard, every strange glance he'd received from his uninterested demeanor... it all started to make sense.

Phantom memories rushed through his mind as he kissed Hephaestion, touching him wherever he could as if he might drown if he couldn't cover every inch of Hephaestion's body in his touch.

"Gods. I can't help it... I just want to fuck her."

"When she kissed me, I almost came then and there. I swear."

"It was the most incredible experience I've ever had."

"I get now why men go to war."

Alexander gasped as Hephaestion picked him up by his thighs and walked them across the room to Alexander's bed.

"Need you," Hephaestion whispered between kisses.

"Yes," Alexander agreed before his back hit the mattress. Hephaestion climbed on top of him and quickly removed his shirt before turning back to Alexander and helping him strip off his own. Alexander gasped quietly as Hephaestion kissed up his chest, licking a stripe over his collarbone and bit his neck. "Ahh..." Alexander moaned, rocking his hips up.

Hephaestion was too far away; Alexander's cock twitched with the lack of pressure and he took Hephaestion's face in his hands, kissing him deeply. With his leg, he pushed Hephaestion's knee, destabilizing him and bringing their hips together once more. They both groaned at the stimulation and Alexander felt his hips thrusting forward on their own. He was no longer second guessing himself, he was hard, he was horny, and he needed Hephaestion.

"Ahh... Hephaestion, please..." Alexander panted, kissing Hephaestion's face before moving down to his neck to suck on his pulse point.

"Mmm... yes, okay... yes..." Hephaestion mumbled, propping himself up with one hand and reaching his other between them, shoving their pants down and freeing their leaking cocks. Alexander almost sobbed when Hephaestion wrapped his hand around both of them and stroked. Alexander threw his head back and cried out, his hips grinding forward into Hephaestion's.

"Fuck," Hephaestion whispered harshly, gripping them more tightly. Alexander wrapped his arms around Hephaestion's broad shoulders and used the leverage to fuck into Hephaestion's fist. It felt so much better than when he'd done it alone in his tent. Hephaestion's hand was larger than his. His smell permeated all of Alexander's senses, and the feeling of Hephaestion's cock sliding against his own left him absolutely wrecked.

Hephaestion rubbed the tip of his cock with his thumb and Alexander jerked his hips forward again. He could feel his climax building and he knew that he wasn't about to last much longer.

"Ahh... Hephaestion... I-I'm close... ahhh..." Alexander mumbled incoherently, breathing heavily.

"Alexander... fuck... Yes, me, too... Shit..." Hephaestion got out through gritted teeth. He gripped them tighter and began stroking faster. Alexander felt his balls tighten as he hung on the edge. Then, as Hephaestion leaned forward and touched his lips to Alexander's ear, he whispered, "A-Alexander..."

Alexander saw white. He came so hard that he felt his spend hit him in the chest. The pleasure spread through his body like a wildfire and his toes curled as it continued. Hephaestion kept milking them until Alexander felt his muscles go rigid above him and heard him moan loudly.

His hips jerked forward a couple more times and his movements became stilted as he came. Once he'd finished, Hep-

CHAPTER THREE 37

haestion leaned down, taking Alexander's face in his hands and kissed him again. It wasn't heated this time, just gentle and satisfied.

Hephaestion shifted slightly to the side and collapsed on the bed next to Alexander. Their breathing was ragged in the quiet of the night and and they lay there in silence for some time. Once Alexander's breathing had returned to normal, he turned his head to look at Hephaestion only to see Hephaestion already watching him.

"That was..." Alexander started, not quite sure what to say.

"Incredible?" Hephaestion finished, grinning widely. Alexander waited a beat to respond and watched Hephaestion's expression waver slightly in nervousness. Alexander smiled softly and reached over, cupping Hephaestion's face in his hand.

"Yes," Alexander whispered. "Incredible."

"Should I...?" Hephaestion asked, his eyes darting to the door, but Alexander shook his head.

"Stay. Please." Hephaestion finally relaxed into the bed and covered Alexander's hand with his own.

They cleaned up and collapsed together, exhausted, into bed. Alexander let his arm float out until it was touching Hephaestion's, eyes closed. He smiled as Hephaestion took his hand in his own and fell into a satisfied, deep sleep.

4

CHAPTER FOUR

When Alexander woke, he thought for a moment that it might have all been a dream. But then he felt it, the strong arms holding him into the warm chest behind him, the legs tangled between his own, and the hot breath tickling the back of his neck.

It hadn't been a dream.

Alexander shifted gently back, further into Hephaestion's embrace, and let himself smile at nothing.

"You awake?" Alexander's eyes popped open at the sound of Hephaestion's sleepy voice.

"Yes," Alexander whispered. Without disturbing the arms around him, Alexander turned around, placing himself nose to nose with Hephaestion. "Hi."

"Hi." Hephaestion murmured. Alexander looked at him for a moment, taking stock of the scene laid out before him: Hephaestion's long eyelashes, his beautiful dark eyes flecked with gold, his plump lips...

Before he registered what he was doing, he pressed his lips against Hephaestion's, desperate to taste him again. He felt Hephaestion's arms tighten around him and his head tilt slightly, slotting their lips together. Alexander sighed into the kiss and let him hands slide up Hephaestion's chest. Hephaestion shifted and Alexander felt a hardness rub up against his thigh; immediately, he began to feel his own cock wake in response.

They kissed softly and slowly at first, which eventually turned into a heavier makeout when Hephaestion used his free hand to cup Alexander's ass. Alexander kissed Hephaestion, rubbing their hips together and moaning softly at each touch. He slid one of his legs between Hephaestion's to get better traction and felt his cock begin to leak.

They were so close together, but not close enough. Alexander snaked his hands up into Hephaestion's hair and pressed their chests together. Maybe they'd cum like this... Maybe Hephaestion would wrap his hand around them again... And maybe he would show him more...

Alexander felt Hephaestion's hand move down to touch them. His thumb brushed over their cocks and-

"Good morning, Alexander!"

Hephaestion and Alexander jumped apart. Alexander grabbed the sheets and piled them on top of his lower half, hiding the proof of their "activities". Hephaestion just looked around in a confused fashion, rubbing his face with one hand.

"You have a packed morning and... Hephaestion?"

"Morning, Thetima." Hephaestion grinned widely, hopping out of the bed and throwing on his clothes from the night before. Alexander sat in bed wide eyed and mortified, barely registering Hephaestion climbing back onto the bed until he turned Alexander's head by the chin and planted a quick kiss on his nose.

"We are talking about this later," Hephaestion promised jovially before hopping out of the bed and saying goodbye to the servants on his way out.

Alexander made eye contact with Thetima, a few beats passing before anything was said. The silence was finally broken as Thetima turned to one of the other female servants.

"You owe me five tetradrachms," Thetima stated boldly to the open-mouthed woman standing next to her. "I told you." Thetima smiled and looked back at Alexander. "I know my boy."

Alexander buried his face in his hands.

After Thetima had finally convinced Alexander to get out of bed, she'd dismissed the rest of the servants and helped him get ready on her own. Luckily for him, she didn't bring up anything about what she'd walked in on; in fact, she seemed completely normal. He'd have to ask her about the exchange of money at a later date, but right now, he was still pretty mortified at the entire situation. After a few more minutes of feeling awkward, Alexander finally let his shoulders relax as Thetima went over the day's schedule with him.

Since they'd just returned from a battle, it wouldn't be too arduous, but because his father had not yet returned and he was still regent, there was plenty to do. Thetima escorted him to the main hall so that he could receive some of his subjects. But before she led him in, she stopped and placed her hands on his shoulders.

"You don't need to feel embarrassed," she started. Thetima had been Alexander's primary servant since he was young; in many ways, she was more of a mother to him than his own had been. "I've known for a long time."

Alexander furrowed his brows, opening and closing his mouth a couple of times. "How?" he asked. "How could you know when I didn't even know?"

Thetima chuckled softly and took his face in her hands. "I am very observant."

Alexander blew air out of his nose in amusement. "Clearly."

"You do not need to explain anything to me. Do not give it a second thought." Thetima smoothed his clothes and finger-brushed some hairs back into place. "Just go be a prince; do what you need to do and speak with Hephaestion later."

Alexander flushed at the last task on her list but nodded dutifully. Thetima pulled him down to her height and kissed him on the forehead, just as she'd done when he was little. As he'd grown, he'd needed to stoop further and further to accommodate her, but he never minded.

"I heard that you were very brave yesterday." Thetima smiled, changing the subject and patting his cheek. Alexander shrugged and grinned back.

"Well, someone's got to protect you, right?"

Thetima laughed loudly and jovially, releasing his face and letting him straighten back up. "True. I am very lucky to have someone like the Prince of Macedon fighting for my safety."

Alexander bid her goodbye and turned to enter the main hall. He really did need to talk to Hephaestion about everything, but his royal duties came first, and Hephaestion knew that. Alexander blushed again, remembering last night, before patting his cheeks to stay the blush, fixing his posture, and walking into the chambers.

CHAPTER FOUR

Alexander was exhausted.

He always forgot how much a fight took out of him in the days following and since he hadn't had a moment to rest since his return, he was certainly feeling that now. He ran his fingers through his hair as he wandered down the hall. He was tired enough that he knew the second his head hit the pillow, he would be asleep, but he hadn't gotten a chance to talk with Hephaestion yet. So, instead of heading back to his quarters, he made his way down the corridor and towards the inner garden.

Turning the corner, he grinned. Hephaestion was sitting under his favorite tree, head lolling as he napped. Alexander stepped into the garden and made his way over to his friend, kneeling next to him. His face was peaceful. Alexander could see every eyelash, every freckle, the slight flush across his cheeks…

Without thinking about it too much, Alexander leaned in and kissed him on the nose. As he pulled away, he was met with sleepy, dark eyes.

"Hey," Hephaestion mumbled sleepily.

"Hey." Alexander smiled and sat down in the grass across from Hephaestion.

"I figured you'd be sleeping by now." Hephaestion adjusted so he was sitting upright against the tree instead of slumped against it. Alexander shrugged and looked down, playing with his fingers.

"Well..." Alexander started. "I wanted to talk to you first."

Alexander looked up to gauge Hephaestion's reaction. He was leaning against the tree with a small smile on his face and a light blush dusting his cheeks.

"Okay."

"Okay." Alexander shifted a little. "Well. I think I owe you some sort of explanation."

"You don't," Hephaestion responded, and Alexander jerked his head up in surprise. "Of course, I want to hear what you have to say, but I don't want you to feel forced into talking about something that would make you uncomfortable. So..." Hephaestion rubbed the back of his neck, blush extending down to his chest. "Just... let's talk to the level that you're comfortable with."

Alexander felt a knot loosen in his chest at Hephaestion's words. Frankly, he didn't really know what he was going to say; he was still figuring out most of this for himself and didn't have an explanation for Hephaestion. So, instead of pushing himself into the conversation, as he'd been prepared to do, he nodded and sat silently for a few minutes to collect his thoughts. Hephaestion sat patiently, waiting for Alexander to begin, but despite knowing that he was being waited on, Alexander didn't feel like he was being pressured. He just felt like Hephaestion valued what he was going to say so much that he would wait as long as Alexander needed... which was so like him.

Alexander cleared his throat. "Last night..."

"Do you regret it?" Hephaestion prompted gently.

"No," Alexander responded quickly, his gaze ascending again to meet Hephaestion's. He wasn't sure, but he thought he saw several layers of distress fall from Hephaestion, his shoulders dropping away from his ears and face relaxing slightly. "Do... Do you?"

Hephaestion grinned. "No."

"Okay." Alexander felt a blush beginning to creep into his cheeks and rubbed them with his palms in an attempt to hide it. Though he knew it was futile anyway; Hephaestion could read him better than anyone else. "I think... maybe... I'd like to do it again?"

Hephaestion's eyebrows shot up. "Really?"

"Really," Alexander replied. Slowly, he scooted closer to Hephaestion until their knees were touching. "I've never really been interested before... in any of that stuff, but..."

"You sure you don't want to try it with someone else?" Alexander almost rejected the offer right off the bat but ultimately decided that it was a fair question and Hephaestion deserved a well thought out answer. So, Alexander thought about it. It was possible that he was just an extremely late bloomer, but he gave the question fair purchase in his mind, thinking about the round breasts of the servant girls, their curvy hips, and long hair and his mouth turned down in distaste. That much hadn't changed, and while he now realized what his taste did consist of, nobody else had ever managed to catch his attention like Hephaestion had.

After several minutes of thinking, Alexander replied, "I'm not interested in that. I don't have any reason to kiss those people. And the idea of doing what we did last night with them..." Alexander's face distorted in disgust. He sighed and swallowed nervously. Maybe Hephaestion wanted to continue to explore with other people, and that's why he was asking. He wanted Alexander to move on so he could keep sleeping around. The thought felt like a rock in Alexander's stomach, but before he could spiral too far down that train of thought, he felt Hephaestion take his hand between his own.

"Me, too," Hephaestion spoke quietly, meeting Alexander's gaze again.

"So," Alexander blinked a couple of times and bit his lip nervously. "I don't want to do that with anyone else... and neither do you."

Hephaestion nodded.

"And... I would like to do it again... with you... And you?"

"I'd like that too, Alexander," Hephaestion responded to the careful question.

"I'm still figuring things out," Alexander warned, not wanting Hephaestion to take his hand back or change his mind, but also not wanting to mislead him.

I know." Hephaestion took his other hand and brought them together in their laps. "Who isn't?"

"And it will just be us?"

"Yes." Hephaestion smiled sweetly. "Are you comfortable with me trying some new things?"

Alexander blushed deeply, thinking of what that could possibly mean, but nodded. He trusted Hephaestion and knew that if he showed any discomfort with anything that was going to happen, Hephaestion would put a stop to it right away. Hephaestion lifted one of Alexander's hands to his mouth and pressed a kiss into his palm, looking to Alexander for his response. Alexander couldn't help it; he felt his heart jump and he blushed again, smiling into his lap.

Then, as if his body knew that the conversation was over, he yawned.

"Tired?" Hephaestion teased.

"Exhausted," Alexander admitted, chuckling lightly.

"You should go to bed. Get some rest," Hephaestion suggested, standing up and pulling Alexander to his feet.

"I know," Alexander groaned as he stood. Hephaestion still had one of Alexander's hands in his own. Alexander chewed the inside of his cheek; he was exhausted, but he didn't want to let go and as if reading Alexander's mind, which Alexander was pretty sure Hephaestion could do at this point, Hephaestion chuckled.

"Come on, I'll walk you."

Alexander smiled and side by side the two young men walked down the hallways. In truth, it wasn't all that different from their typical routine, except for the comforting warmth of Hephaestion's hand in his own. They walked in silence all the way back, not crossing another soul the entire way there. In a way, Alexander was grateful for that. He didn't want to let go of Hephaestion's hand, but he'd denied companions for so long that he was sure people would stare, and he wasn't confident that he was ready for that.

As they approached Alexander's room, Hephaestion squeezed their hands and let go. Immediately, Alexander felt the absence of where Hephaestion's hand used to be and he closed his hand in on itself to fill it.

"I should probably sleep, too." Hephaestion smiled. "Sleep well, Alexander."

"Um," Alexander called out as Hephaestion turned to go. "You know, I slept pretty well last night."

Hephaestion turned back to look at him, his eyebrows raised slightly.

"So, if you didn't want to go back to your room... you could... um... sleep here... again," Alexander offered, looking everywhere except at Hephaestion for a few moments of silence. After receiving no response, Alexander looked back over at his friend. Hephaestion was smiling softly, his face glowing in the candlelight.

"I think I'd like that."

"Me too." Alexander nodded and held the door open. Hephaestion followed Alexander inside and closed the door gently behind them. Alexander turned his attention to his dresser as he disrobed, pulling his shirt over his head and setting it on the surface. Before he had a chance to take off his pants, he felt Hephaestion's rough hands wrap their way around his torso from behind.

He sighed and leaned back into Hephaestion's chest, his own arms overlapping Hephaestion's. The taller man nuzzled his face into the crook of Alexander's neck and pressed a couple of chaste kisses into the skin. Alexander felt himself relax and he realized that he'd been waiting for this all day. He'd never had trouble sleeping before, but somehow he knew that if Hephaestion hadn't been here with him tonight, he would have slept fitfully at best.

"Mmm," Alexander vocalized, tilting his head slightly to give Hephaestion better access. Hephaestion nipped gently at his neck and pressed more kisses into his skin before taking Alexander by the waist and turning him around. Alexander instinctively moved forward to meet Hephaestion's lips, relishing the feeling of Hephaestion's hands on his bare skin.

"I know you're tired," Hephaestion murmured between kisses. "So, I wanted to do something for you tonight." Alexander's breath hitched as he felt one of Hephaestion's hands slide down his back and cup his ass. "That alright?"

Alexander nodded. "Yes." Hephaestion smiled into the kiss and pulled off his own shirt, tossing it somewhere off to the side and backed them up to the bed, sitting Alexander down before dropping to his knees. "What are you doing?" Alexander asked, confused.

"Do you trust me?" As Hephaestion replied with his own question. Alexander chuckled softly, of course he did. So, he nodded. Hephaestion nodded in return before tucking his fingers into the waist of Alexander's pants and pulling them down below Alexander's balls, freeing his mostly flaccid cock. Then, without further explanation, Hephaestion took Alexander's cock into his mouth, sucking tightly and swirling his tongue around the head.

Alexander's head dropped back as he moaned out in pleasure. He could feel his cock filling with each suck and stroke of Hephaestion's mouth and hands. Despite feeling nearly boneless, Alexander forced himself to lift his head back up so he could see Hephaestion taking him into his mouth over and over again. At the sight, he felt himself become fully erect, twitching slightly. He didn't think he had ever seen anything quite so arousing in his entire life.

Hephaestion's piercing eyes were trained on Alexander as he watched every movement, every reaction, to what he was doing. Hephaestion pulled back and kissed the tip before sucking gently on the head. Alexander felt his eyes roll back into his head, and just when he didn't think that it could get any better, Hephaestion took his full length into his mouth. Tears pricked at the corners of his eyes as Alexander's cock hit the back of his throat and as Hephaestion began swallowing around his dick, Alexander felt his orgasm building rapidly.

Looking back down at Hephaestion, Alexander noticed his arm moving beneath them. He had to bite his lip to prevent himself from coming right then and there as he realized Hephaestion had pulled his own leaking cock out of his pants and was pleasuring himself to the act of sucking Alexander off.

"Fuck," Alexander groaned. "Hephaestion... I... I'm gonna cum..."

Hephaestion hummed in acknowledgment, but did not pull off. Instead, he opted to speed up his work, sucking and swallowing around Alexander at an even more punishing pace. Alexander's breath hitched as he felt himself falling over the edge. He reached out one hand and grabbed Hephaestion's shoulder to ground himself. As his orgasm rushed through him, he came directly down Hephaestion's throat and Hephaestion swallowed it down greedily.

As Hephaestion continued suck Alexander through his climax, Alexander felt him grab his calf and stutter his hips as he stroked his cock, cumming on the floor.

"Ahhhhh," Alexander moaned, rolling his hips forward instinctively to milk every last second of his orgasm. It felt like Hephaestion had sucked his soul out of his body; he'd never felt so satisfied in his entire life. Hephaestion pulled off and climbed up onto the bed, kissing Alexander deeply. He could taste himself on Hephaestion's lips, but he couldn't bring himself to care. Alexander threaded his fingers into Hephaestion's hair and kissed him back like his life depended on it.

"So, how was that?" Hephaestion murmured against Alexander's lips.

CHAPTER FOUR 53

"You're joking right?" Alexander chuckled. "That was incredible."

Hephaestion smiled into the kiss before standing back up and pulling his pants off. "Come on, I'm sure you're ready to sleep."

Alexander nodded, still lying back on the bed, cock not yet put away. Hephaestion laughed, helping Alexander out of his pants before crawling under the covers and pulling Alexander with him. Alexander sighed and relaxed into Hephaestion's embrace, feeling his warmth pressed up against his back. "Night..." Alexander mumbled as his consciousness faded.

"Night, Alexander." Hephaestion leaned in and pressed a couple of kisses to Alexander's neck. Alexander was absolutely sure he'd died and gone to heaven. He smiled to himself as he fell asleep that night, pressed against Hephaestion.

CHAPTER FIVE

The first thing Alexander registered when he woke up was that he was not alone. Blood rushed to his face as he remembered the events from the night before. Hephaestion had not only wanted to continue what they were doing, but he had gotten off to sucking Alexander's cock mere hours ago. Alexander grinned and turned over so he could see his bed companion.

Hephaestion's hair was messy and ruffled from sleep; he always looked adorable while sleeping. But now that Alexander knew he was allowed to look, he took his time. His lips were slightly parted and still pink from their escapades the night before. His eyelashes were long and cast shadows on his cheeks in the morning sun that trickled through the window. He lay on his side, muscular shoulders and arms toned and gorgeous despite being at rest.

Alexander let his eyes wander down to Hephaestion's tapered waist and to his v-line. In the night, the covers had slid down so that his lower-half was barely covered. In fact, the sheet hung so low that Alexander could see the tip of Hephaestion's morning wood, standing strong against the linen. Immediately, Alexander felt his own cock stir and he blushed deeper; he'd never been a horny or perverted person, but as if some sort of dam had broken the very first night he'd kissed Hephaestion, he couldn't help but get hard when thinking about him.

Alexander ran his hand down his bedmate's chest as he remembered how Hephaestion had gotten down on his knees for him. Gently, he pulled the sheet down further, fully exposing Hephaestion's erect cock.

He wondered how he tasted…

Taking one more cursory look up to Hephaestion's sleeping face, Alexander slid down until his face was level with the erect length. Alexander stuck his tongue out and licked a stripe up Hephaestion's cock, from base to tip. Hephaestion shifted slightly in his sleep but did not wake up.

Alexander wrapped his hand around the base of Hephaestion's cock and took the head into his mouth. He knew that he probably couldn't take all of him into his mouth as Hephaestion had done to him the night before, but he shuddered remembering how amazing it had felt. He wanted to give Hephaestion the same amazing feeling.

Slowly Alexander began to suck, hollowing his cheeks out and sucking on the tip, using his hand to stroke the rest of it to the same rhythm. Hephaestion's hips began to rock slightly in turn with Alexander's ministrations and a few pleasured noises escaped his throat in his sleep.

Gaining confidence, Alexander began using his tongue to swirl around the length as he sucked, stroking even more firmly with his hand.

"Ahh... fu... mmm..." Hephaestion began to stir from his sleep, his hand traveling down to his hips, fingertips meeting Alexander's hair. "A... mmm... Alexander?"

Alexander hummed at Hephaestion's sleepy realization and continued to suck, the salty taste of precum hitting his tongue. Hephaestion's breath began to pick up and his hips continued to rock, chasing the warm feeling of Alexander's mouth.

"Ff-fuck... Alexander... Ah... mmm... I'm not gonna last... shit..." Alexander prepared himself for what he knew was coming and continued sucking, this time taking as much as he could into his mouth without gagging. "Ahhh... oh, fuck..."

Alexander felt Hephaestion tense, his abs rippling as they clenched, a pleasured moan escaping from his lips. Alexander felt Hephaestion's cock throb as his cum flooded into Alexander's mouth. Repeating Hephaestion's performance from the night prior, Alexander swallowed it as best as he could before pulling off and scooting back up to the pillows.

Hephaestion took his face in his hands and planted a kiss right on Alexander's lips. "That was the hottest thing I've ever experienced." Hephaestion let his tongue wander into Alexander's mouth, his arms wrapping around his torso, pulling him in so their bodies were flush with one another. "You're so sexy," Hephaestion murmured, letting his kisses move from Alexander's lips to his earlobe and then down his neck.

As Alexander pressed his body into Hephaestion's, he noticed his own hardness, pressing up against Hephaestion's hip. He had been enjoying the noises Hephaestion had been making so much that he had completely forgotten about his own arousal. He gasped as he felt Hephaestion's hand worm its way between them and wrap around his dick.

Hephaestion kept kissing his neck and collarbone as he began stroking him. Alexander had already gotten so worked up from making Hephaestion cum that his cock was already leaking. Hephaestion gathered some of that precum with his fingers and used it to lube up Alexander's length. Alexander wrapped his arms around Hephaestion's neck, thrusting into Hephaestion's grip. It began slowly at first, leisurely kisses and slow, deliberate strokes, but quickly devolved into desperate, messy thrusts and wet, intense kisses.

Alexander fucked into Hephaestion's fist until he felt himself spill, letting out a shuddering breath. Hephaestion leaned over to the side, wiped his hand on his tunic laying on the floor and turned back around to face Alexander, kissing him on the nose.

They lay in silence for a while as Alexander caught his breath. Then, as he opened his eyes, he met Hephaestion's gaze.

"This isn't a dream, is it?" Hephaestion asked quietly.

Alexander smiled and dragged his thumb across Hephaestion's cheek. "No. It's not a dream."

"You really want me like this?"

"I really want you like this," Alexander replied, leaning forward and kissing Hephaestion on the lips; and as they lay there, everything felt right in the world, like nothing could go wrong.

Yet, as he sat in the throne room the next day, listening to the pleas and complaints of the populace, he felt a chill go up his spine when his father's guard interrupted the session, clearing out the room. Once everyone was gone, the door swung open again and he stood as Thetima entered the space.

"Thetima." Alexander made his way over to the woman as quickly as he could. "What is going on?"

Thetima stood stoically in the throne room, collecting herself; Alexander had known something was wrong as soon as the guards had cut short the session and sent away his subjects, but Thetima's reaction to his question just confirmed it.

Thetima took a deep breath and lifted her head, meeting his gaze. "Your father is dead, Alexander."

"What do you mean he's dead?" He hadn't been fighting, he was at Cleopatra's wedding. It made absolutely no sense that he would be dead. Immediately, he felt Hephaestion's hand take his own; he didn't need to look to know that the worried frown he wore sometimes would be on his face. "Wasn't he just at Cleopatra's wedding?"

Thetima pursed her lips and looked away, gathering herself. "He was assassinated."

Alexander felt his heart drop into his ass. "What?"

"He was mostly unprotected because he was with foreign dignitaries and in the company of friends and family."

"Where were his guards?" Alexander demanded, feeling his throat begin to close as tears threatened to spill from his eyes.

Thetima sniffed and looked directly at the floor. "They were there."

"Thetima... I don't understand..."

"It was Pausinias." Alexander's eyes grew to the size of saucers and he could swear his heart stopped for a moment.

"Pausinias... one of my father's guards assassinated him?"

"Yes," Thetima whispered, finally looking up to meet Alexander's gaze. Her eyes were misty but her face was steely as if she was trying to be strong for the both of them. Alexander noticed that her eyes were already puffy as if she had already been crying on her way over to tell him. Hephaestion squeezed Alexander's hand and Alexander realized he'd been silent for far too long.

"Where is he?" Alexander demanded. Thetima pursed her lips again.

"Your father's body is on the way back to the royal tombs at Vergina for burial preparation... and Pausinias... is awaiting sentencing upon his arrival back here."

Alexander felt his chest clench. His father's body. It had such a finality to it.

He'd seen his father not too long ago, alive and fighting alongside him. It seemed almost surreal to think about the fact that he was gone. But, almost more baffling was the fact that it had been Pausinias, one of his father's most trusted guards, who'd done him in.

"What will be done with him?" Alexander questioned.

CHAPTER FIVE

"Well." Thetima swallowed. "That's up to you."

"What?" Alexander lifted his head to meet Thetima's gaze.

"With your father gone, Alexander, that makes you King of Macedon."

With your father gone...

King of Macedon...

Alexander blinked, bringing himself back into the moment. That was how it worked wasn't it? The reason that his father had taken so many wives and women was to produce a male heir that would take over upon his death. This was why he had been taught and trained from such a young age... to be the king his father wanted him to be when he left it all behind.

In the confused haze, he remembered something his father had said to him not two weeks ago.

Macedon is far too small for you.

Alexander remembered the smile on his father's face as he'd said it.

You will find an empire fit for you one day, Alexander, fit for you and your talents.

His vision began to blur, he was only 20... he wasn't ready to run the empire. If he became king... If it really was time, that meant...

Alexander knew what was expected of him.

When Alexander blinked, he felt wetness run down his cheeks. Bringing his hand up, he swiped his fingertips across his cheek... Tears...

He opened his mouth to speak, only for nothing to come out. Only silence.

"Alexander..." Hephaestion whispered, wrapping an arm around his shoulders. Alexander looked over to his best friend, eyeing him with concern. Suddenly, their bubble was popped by the sound of the door opening.

"Apologies, my King."

My King.

Alexander turned to see Regulus, the head of his father's guard, entering the room and bowing deeply. "I understand that the news was just delivered to you. However, the traitor is awaiting your sentencing in the palace cells."

"Now?" Alexander pulled together all his courage to ask that one question. When the head guard nodded, Alexander pursed his lips, gathering himself. "Hephaestion."

"Yes." Hephaestion was in front of him before he could ask the question.

"Fetch my sword."

Hephaestion's eyes went wide, lips parting like he wanted to say something but thought better of it. "Yes, my King."

Alexander turned to Regulus as Hephaestion walked quickly out of the room. "Lead the way."

He took a step following the guards when he felt a small hand on his arm. He turned and saw Thetima, eyes wide like she couldn't believe she'd stopped him. "I'm so…"

"It's fine." Alexander let the words rush out of him quickly. "I'll handle it."

Thetima looked at the floor then back up to Alexander, seeming conflicted. "It doesn't seem right that you should have to deal with this right now."

"I know," Alexander responded, shrugging his shoulders. "But this is what I've been trained for. I'm a King now."

Thetima's brows furrowed, a single tear escaping the corner of her eye.

"It will be fine, really." Alexander patted Thetima's hand before letting it slip away. Once she let it go, he turned and followed the guard down the hall and towards the cells.

His footsteps echoed down the marble hallway and he was only vaguely aware of the guards surrounding him. It made sense, he supposed. He was the new King and the previous King had just been assassinated. Of course, they'd raise security; they wanted to protect their new ruler.

At least until he produced an heir...

The thought made Alexander's stomach twist in discomfort. He adjusted his gait, steering himself towards the door, stepped outside, and vomited everything that had been in his stomach into the bushes lining the building. He coughed a couple of times, spitting, and forcing himself to breathe.

"Are you alright, Sire?" Regulus asked. Alexander steeled himself through a second wave of nausea. He couldn't think about that right now. He had a job to do.

Alexander stood back up straight and wiped his mouth with the back of his hand. "Yes. Let's go." He turned back around to head inside; Regulus had a look of concern etched into his face, weathered by war, but simply nodded and continued down the hallway. When they turned the corner to the holding cells, Alexander sighed a small breath of relief because there at the door was Hephaestion, and he was holding Alexander's sword. Alexander could see that it was taking everything in him not to run over and throw his arms around him, but now was hardly the time, and they both knew it.

Alexander had to do his duty and his guard needed to see him acting as a King would, not running into the arms of his...

His...

Hephaestion locked eyes with him and nodded in encouragement. As they approached the door, Hephaestion held out Alexander's sword to him, falling into step after him once he took it. Several guards held the doors open and Alexander strode in, walking directly up to the man tied to the jail wall, hanging by his arms.

"Alexander..." Pausinias lifted his head, recognition in his eyes. But upon locking eyes with Alexander's furious gaze, he looked away guiltily to the side of the cell.

"Leave us," Alexander spoke in a commanding voice fit for a King.

"Ale... my King," Regulus warned. "I don't think that's a good idea. He just killed your father, he's dangerous."

"I don't believe I asked for your opinion, Regulus," Alexander responded coldly. "Hephaestion will stay with me."

Alexander stood in the silence of the space while he waited for Regulus' response. He could hear the gears turning in the other man's head. Regulus had known Alexander since he was a child and cared for him like Thetima did, but he also knew that he couldn't stand against the new King without causing a myriad of problems. "Yes Sire," Regulus finally said, sounding tired.

"Alexander... I-" Pausinias began, but he was cut off.

"You fucking look at me while you are speaking to me!" Alexander shouted, his Kingly facade cracking. Pausinias flinched, his eyes darting away and back again almost as if he lost his nerve to look Alexander in the face every two seconds.

"No, you can't," Alexander growled. "Do you realize what you've done?"

Pausinias pursed his lips. "Yes... you're the King now. Isn't that a good... thing? Ack!!!"

Alexander grabbed him by the throat in a crushing grip. "Isn't that a good thing? *Really?* That's what you're going with?"

Alexander released Pausinias and stepped back, disgust on his face as Pausinias coughed and spat in an attempt to catch his breath, struggling to do so while bound.

"Your father..." Pausinias started again with a raspy voice. "He was a tyrant; it wasn't just me who thought so..."

Crack!

Alexander's strike made a sickening crack as his rings broke several of Pausinias's teeth.

"He *trusted* you. How could you?" Alexander wheezed, unable to breathe properly.

"I thought that the empire would be better off with you in charge," Pausinias replied, spitting out some of his teeth and wincing in pain. "Am I supposed to apologize for putting you in power?" he spat.

Alexander saw red.

Before he knew what was happening, his body acted, drawing his sword and piercing Pausinias through the chest. The look of surprise on the guard's face said it all. Alexander was not a violent person; while his father had been known to execute traitors by his own hand, Alexander had never had the taste for it, always looking away.

"You..." Alexander whispered, tears streaming down his cheeks. "You cannot understand... what you have done..."

Alexander twisted the sword, pulling it out as he watched the light fade from Pausinias's eyes.

Slowly, Hephaestion's voice began breaking through the sound of blood pounding through Alexander's ears.

"...der ...lexander ... Alexander."

"What?" Alexander turned, returning back to the moment to see a concerned Hephaestion reaching out to grip him by the shoulders.

"Alexander... are you-" Then as if realizing how idiotic of a question it would be to ask him, he stopped. "Stay here."

Alexander stood, sword hanging down by his legs as he heard Hephaestion open the door and speak to Regulus in hushed voices.

"The traitor is dead. I am taking Alexander back to his chambers. Please handle this mess."

"Yes, Master Hephaestion... and..."

"Yes?"

"Take care of him."

"I will."

A couple of moments later, Alexander felt Hephaestion's warm arms wrap around him, leading him out through the back door and into the night.

Chapter Six

Alexander wasn't sure how they got back to his chambers. The night was a blur of columns passing, the sound of trees rustling, and servants whispering. All he registered when the door to his chambers closed was Hephaestion's hand on his own, gently straightening his fingers to take the sword he had been clutching since the execution. Alexander let go, allowing Hephaestion to take the sword and place it somewhere behind them.

He felt Hephaestion's hands find his shoulders again and lead him back into his bathing area. He vaguely registered the sound of water running and the smell of his favorite soap; but he was still in such a fog that he couldn't move, let alone begin undressing. As if understanding this, Hephaestion began gently taking Alexander's clothes off, placing them to the side, and holding him in a comforting fashion. He saw Hephaestion's lips moving but he couldn't hear what he was saying.

I'm sorry, he wanted to say, but his lips wouldn't move. So he didn't.

Instead, he let himself be led into the water, the warmth traveling up his legs and torso until he was sitting, chest-deep in the bath. He felt loving hands rubbing all over his body, cleaning off the blood and dirt, and blocking his eyes as warm bathwater was poured onto his hair.

Hephaestion massaged Alexander's scalp, taking extra care to ensure that no blood remained on his face from the execution. Slowly, Alexander began to come back into himself.

"It is going to be okay Alexander," he heard Hephaestion whispering as he ran his fingers through the blonde's hair. Slowly he raised his eyes to meet Hephaestion's gaze. "Alexander?" Hephaestion asked, searching his eyes for recognition. "Alexander, can you hear me?"

Alexander blinked. He still couldn't find his voice, but he could feel his body again, so he just nodded.

"Oh, thank the gods," Hephaestion mumbled, his voice breaking slightly. He pulled Alexander into a hug, burying his face in Alexander's wet shoulder. Alexander lifted his arms and wrapped them around Hephaestion's back. It felt good to be held like this; he felt safe... like everything was going to be okay. Alexander sighed, gripping Hephaestion's wet shirt.

"Hephaestion," Alexander tried, his voice tired and creaky. Hephaestion pulled back, his hands still on Alexander's shoulders.

"Yes?"

"Why are you in your clothes?" Alexander frowned, clutching the shirt. Hephaestion smiled, a few tears escaping his eyes.

"You couldn't get in the water by yourself, so I just got in with you." Hephaestion chuckled softly, cupping Alexander's face in his hand as if he was afraid that Alexander was going to slip away from him again.

"I see," Alexander responded. Now feeling a bit more in control of his body, he reached down to grab the bottom of Hephaestion's shirt, pulling it over his head.

"Alexander, what are you..." Hephaestion started but stopped again as Alexander just shook his head, tossing the shirt to the side.

"You're in the bath now, might as well get clean." Alexander did his best to smile a little. Hephaestion blew air out of his nose in a quick laugh.

"Yeah, I suppose you're right," Hephaestion murmured. He moved Alexander off his lap for a moment so he could remove his pants, plopping them on the floor next to his shirt. Then, he pulled Alexander back into his lap, their chests touching and Alexander's legs wrapped around Hephaestion's back.

Alexander rested his head on Hephaestion's shoulder as they embraced. This could have easily been a sexual thing, but it just wasn't. It was comforting, intimate, and loving. Hephaestion let his hand run up and down Alexander's back, spilling water over his shoulders with each movement to keep him warm. Alexander wanted to stay like this forever, but he was fading fast.

"Hephaestion..." Alexander murmured.

"Yes?"

"Can we go to bed?" There it was. Alexander was far too tired to think about the implications of what his question meant. They hadn't slept together; in fact, there was nothing sexual about the situation they were both in, but still. Alexander wanted to sleep tonight wrapped in Hephaestion's arms.

Hephaestion pulled back slowly, cupping Alexander's face and giving him a soft kiss. "Of course."

Alexander nodded and allowed himself to be led out of the bath, where Hephaestion dried him off, taking special care to make sure his hair was dry enough that he wouldn't get sick. Then, Hephaestion took his hand and led him to the bed; gently, he pulled back the bedding and helped Alexander lie down. Alexander was briefly worried that Hephaestion had misunderstood, that he would leave and go to his own bedroom, but that worry was short-lived.

Hephaestion blew out the candles in the room and climbed into bed right next to Alexander, wrapping his arms around the blonde and pressing his lips into the golden locks.

CHAPTER SIX

"Hephaestion?" Alexander spoke into the darkness, his face pressed into Hephaestion's chest.

"Yes, Alexander?" Hephaestion replied softly.

"I... I'm afraid," Alexander admitted. He was raised to live life fearlessly, attacking each moment as it came to him, pressing forward. But in the dark of the room, being held by Hephaestion, Alexander let himself admit his fear out loud.

"I know." Hephaestion hugged him tighter and tangled their legs together. "But, Alexander... I promise... we are going to get through this together, okay?"

Alexander felt a few fresh tears slide from his eyes and drip from his nose. "Okay."

Alexander woke up feeling like he'd been run over by a chariot. His head was throbbing and his stomach was incredibly queasy, but as he turned, he felt a sense of relief wash through him. He was now nose to nose with Hephaestion, who had stayed the entire night with him, just holding him, to make sure he was okay. So much had changed in the past 24 hours, but at least that had stayed the same.

Alexander reached out and took Hephaestion's hand in his, pressing his lips to the sleeping man's. As he pulled back, he was met with the beautiful dark eyes he adored so much.

"Alexander," Hephaestion mumbled, voice still thick with sleep. He brought his free hand up to Alexander's face and ran his palm over his cheek. "How are you feeling?"

Alexander shrugged. "Like shit."

Hephaestion snorted. "I guess that is to be expected." Alexander smiled a little, squeezing Hephaestion's hand. "I don't think anyone expects you to be up and about this morning. Not until the naming, later this afternoon, so... do you want to just stay in bed?"

Alexander shook his head. "I don't want to be anywhere near this place while the preparations are happening. Let's go for a walk."

Hephaestion nodded and pressed a kiss to Alexander's forehead before sitting up and swinging his legs off of the bed. Alexander followed suit and sat up, rubbing his eyes as his head throbbed. He heard a plop of something land next to him and when he opened his eyes, he saw that he had been tossed some clothes. He smiled in thanks and pulled the clothes on, watching as Hephaestion did the same.

"Where do you want to go?" Hephaestion asked.

CHAPTER SIX

Alexander thought for a moment. "Take me to the sea."

Hephaestion smiled and nodded, extending his hand. Alexander took it and followed him to the stables where they saddled up their horses and took off for the coastline. It wasn't that far of a ride, but it was long enough that Alexander could actually feel like they were getting away from it all. When the ocean rose to meet the horizon, they slowed their horses to a trot to look for a place to stop.

They found it pretty quickly: a little beach, hidden from the rest of the coastline and blocked by rocks. Hephaestion and Alexander tied their horses to a log that had washed up onto the shore and walked out to look at the water. Alexander took off his shoes and waded into the sea up to his ankles, letting the water lap over his feet. He didn't need to look to know that Hephaestion was doing the same. Ever since they were kids, they'd both loved the water. And even though they hadn't been in quite some time, he was sure Hephaestion remembered.

"I don't want to get married," Alexander admitted, still gazing out at the ocean. "I know I'm supposed to get married, take women, and have heirs, but..."

"I know." Hephaestion reached out and took Alexander's hand in his own.

"I was supposed to have more time..." Alexander felt tears welling up in his eyes again. "More time to just... be, with you."

Alexander turned his head to see Hephaestion already looking at him, eyes glassy. "Me, too."

Alexander blinked and several tears ran down his cheeks. Hephaestion pulled him in and wrapped his arms around Alexander's waist. "We *will* figure this out, okay?" Hephaestion promised.

Alexander nodded, wanting to believe him. The taller man pulled Alexander tighter and kissed him, his lips salty from the ocean air. Alexander let his hands wander up the back of Hephaestion's shirt and gripped it between his shoulders. He leaned into the kiss, tilting his head slightly so their lips were better slotted together.

Hephaestion kissed him slowly, sucking on his lower lip, then moving back to just kissing him; opening his mouth and letting his tongue touch Alexander's lips. The kiss was different than any other kiss they'd had up to this point. It was slow, not leading to anything. It was as if they were both content just to kiss and hold each other without the exception for anything more.

It was sweet, and Alexander wanted more of it. "I don't want to stop this," Alexander whispered against Hephaestion's lips.

"Me neither," Hephaestion replied, kissing Alexander once more. "Maybe we don't have to…"

CHAPTER SIX

Alexander looked up, his brows furrowed. Was that really a possibility?

As if reading his mind, Hephaestion responded. "I mean, your father was married to multiple women and still took concubines on the side. Who's to say that we can't keep doing what we are doing, despite you needing to produce an heir?"

Alexander opened and closed his mouth in surprise. "I suppose... no one."

"Exactly." Hephaestion grinned. "Besides, you're the King now. What are they going to do? Tell on you?"

Alexander giggled, feeling more hopeful than he had since he'd received the news about his father. "You're right..." Alexander realized. "I am the King. People have to listen to what I say."

Hephaestion nodded confidently, hugging Alexander tighter. "I promised everything was going to be okay, didn't I?"

Alexander smiled. "Yes."

"And have I ever lied to you?" Hephaestion prompted, one eyebrow raised.

"No," Alexander replied, smiling back.

Things were going to be okay; he wasn't going to have to continue on without Hephaestion. He still had no idea what exactly any of this meant, but he had been devastated at the idea of not being able to find out. Sure, he would need to find a wife and produce an heir, and yes, the idea of sleeping with anyone other than Hephaestion still made him a little sick to his stomach, but there was light at the end of the tunnel now.

Alexander buried his head in the crook of Hephaestion's neck and hugged him tightly. "Thank you."

"Of course," Hephaestion whispered, kissing his head. "Anything for you."

The two spent the rest of the morning sitting on the beach and spending time together, just the two of them. Alexander knew that the time for leisure would be over as soon as they arrived back at the palace, and he just wanted to soak up as much time as he could before everything got turned upside down.

"Hephaestion." Alexander traced the veins in Hephaestion's hand as they sat side by side in the sand.

"Hm?" Hephaestion replied, turning to look over at Alexander.

"What is this?" Alexander asked, meeting Hephaestion's gaze.

"What do you mean?" Hephaestion responded, squeezing Alexander's hand.

"Are we just having sex?" Alexander continued, drawing up all the courage he could muster. "Or is this something... else?"

Ever since last night, after being informed of his father's assassination, he'd begun to think about the nature of his and Hephaestion's relationship. He knew that Hephaestion was more experienced in these things, and for that he was grateful, but he was also worried. He'd considered that this might have just been another hookup for Hephaestion and the thought had made him incredibly uneasy. He wasn't quite sure why; he just knew that he needed to know, one way or the other.

He didn't know what he was going to do with the information once he got it, but for some reason, despite everything going on, what with his father's death and his new title, all he could think about was Hephaestion.

"Well," Hephaestion feigned deep thought, "technically, we haven't had sex yet, so..."

Alexander laughed and punched him in the shoulder. "You know what I mean, asshole."

Hephaestion laughed along with Alexander before swallowing and taking a deep breath. "Is that what you want?" Alexander almost argued that he'd asked first, but the words caught in his throat as he saw Hephaestion chew his bottom lip - a telltale sign that he was nervous.

"I..." Alexander started. "I know you have more experience than me, and when I think about the idea that I'm just a number... It makes me..." Alexander searched for the right word. "Sad?"

Hephaestion lifted his eyes back up to Alexander's face, some relief crossing over his features. Hephaestion pulled Alexander over so he was straddling Hephaestion's lap again. It was very similar to the position they'd sat in together while bathing the night before.

"You're not just a number to me, Alexander," Hephaestion confessed, taking the blonde's face in his hands and kissing him deeply. "I care about you... a lot, and I didn't say anything because I didn't want to scare you." Hephaestion ran his hand through Alexander's hair lovingly. "You've never shown any interest in anyone before and I wanted to take things day by day."

Alexander smiled. "I care about you, too." Alexander wrapped his legs around Hephaestion's torso and buried his face in the taller man's neck, breathing in the familiar, comforting scent. "I think I might have never shown interest in anyone else because I already had you, so..."

Hephaestion squeezed Alexander tightly. "Okay."

"Okay," Alexander nodded, feeling more at ease than he had felt in the last couple of days.

7

CHAPTER SEVEN

When they arrived back at the palace, the whole place was bustling with energy. Everyone was preparing for the naming of Alexander as the new King of Macedon, so nobody even noticed when the two men snuck past the front entryway and back into Alexander's chambers.

With newfound confidence at Hephaestion's confession, Alexander closed the door and pressed them up against the wall, kissing him passionately. Immediately he felt Hephaestion's body respond: his breath hitching, his hands taking their place on Alexander's hips, and his cock stirring. Alexander wound his fingers into Hephaestion's black hair and pressed their hips together, grinding slowly.

Alexander felt himself harden as Hephaestion moved one hand to his ass and moaned softly, grinding back into him. Alexander could feel Hephaestion's length up against his hips; with one hand, Alexander gripped Hephaestion through his clothes, relishing the soft gasp that came with the action. Moving his lips down to Hephaestion's neck, Alexander began to bite and suck, leaving red marks in his wake.

He'd learned the very first night they'd been together that Hephaestion had a sensitive neck and that he loved it when Alexander gave it special attention. Alexander palmed Hephaestion's now fully erect cock through his clothes, still grinding his hips on Hephaestion's thigh. Hephaestion squeezed Alexander's ass and moved his hand lower, dipping slightly under. Alexander gasped as Hephaestion's fingers prodded at his hole through his clothes.

"Fuck. Alexander..." Hephaestion was panting now. "Can I show you something new?"

Alexander swallowed. This was unexplored territory, but he had told Hephaestion that he wanted to learn from him and gods, did he want to do everything under the sun with this man. "Yes, just..."

"We'll go slow," Hephaestion promised, switching positions with the blonde. Alexander nodded and allowed himself to be pushed up against the wall, chest and cheek kissing the marble. He could no longer see Hephaestion, but he could hear him as his knees hit the floor. Alexander's breath hitched as Hephaestion pulled his pants down to his ankles and began kissing his ass cheeks.

Alexander's erection bobbed, precum beginning to accumulate at the tip. Hephaestion got closer and closer to the top of

Alexander's thighs when he finally spread them open, licking a stripe over his hole. Alexander gasped, knees buckling slightly but Hephaestion kept to his promise, moving slowly as he kissed and licked, eating Alexander out. Just when Alexander had gotten used to the feeling of Hephaestion's tongue, he gasped again as Hephaestion poked his tongue past the tight ring of muscle.

Alexander took a moment to get used to the intrusion; it was strange, but he didn't hate it - he was still hard, after all. As Hephaestion continued, he wrapped his large hands around Alexander's hips, close enough to Alexander's cock to be tantalizing, but not close enough for any relief.

"He... Hephaestion... please..." Alexander begged. Hephaestion paused only for a moment before Alexander felt a single finger pressing into his hole. There wasn't much resistance as Hephaestion had already opened Alexander up by tongue-fucking him, but Alexander still cried out when Hephaestion sunk down to his knuckle. "Hephaestion... Hephaestion..." Alexander chanted, desperate for some sort of relief.

"Hang on," Hephaestion cooed, twisting his finger around as if he was searching for something. "It's around here somewhere..."

Hephaestion pressed down and Alexander felt a wave of pleasure rush through his body unlike anything he'd ever experienced before. "Ahhhh!" Alexander moaned loudly, unconsciously pushing back onto Hephaestion's finger.

"There it is." Alexander could hear the smile in his voice as Hephaestion began to rub that spot relentlessly. Quickly, Alexander felt himself reaching the edge, his cock was angry red and dripping with precum. He was about to reach down and touch himself when Hephaestion leaned in and bit his ass.

Alexander came, hard.

His orgasm came in waves, each wave shooting more cum onto the marble floor, and the entire time, Hephaestion worked him through it. He kept rubbing that spot inside Alexander and peppering kisses all over Alexander's ass and thighs. When his orgasm finally came to an end, he felt his knees buckle again, but luckily, Hephaestion was there to steady him. He pulled his finger out and hugged Alexander tightly so he wouldn't fall.

Once Alexander had caught his breath, he turned around and kissed the taller man. "Gods Hephaestion, what was that?"

"That," Hephaestion explained, "is the primary reason men like to take it up the ass."

Alexander blushed and hid his face in Hephaestion's shoulder, eliciting a laugh from him. "If only your Kingdom could see you now. What would they say, I wonder?" Hephaestion teased.

Alexander half-heartedly smacked Hephaestion on the chest. "Oh shut up. I bet you'd like it too."

Hephaestion took Alexander's chin and tilted his head up so Alexander could meet his gaze. "Oh, I do."

Alexander blushed harder at the implication of the comment, his dick twitching in interest again. Hephaestion laughed and tugged Alexander over to the bath. The naming ceremony was going to begin soon and they were covered in sand and saltwater. Alexander followed Hephaestion into the bath and settled down next to him, allowing Hephaestion to wash his back and hair like he had the night before.

However, this time, there was no pretext that Alexander could not do it himself. Alexander meant something to Hephaestion and now that it was out there, Hephaestion seemed determined to show it. After the soap was gone, Hephaestion pulled Alexander back into his lap and began planting kisses all over his body.

"Alexander…" Hephaestion murmured between kisses. "You're so beautiful."

Alexander flushed, not knowing what to say, so instead, he wrapped his arms around Hephaestion and began kissing his neck. Hephaestion let out a satisfied sigh and pulled Alexander as close as he could.

Hephaestion was still half hard from their prior activities and his cock very quickly filled up with Alexander on top of him, lavishing his neck. Alexander could feel his length between them and moved his hips slowly, rubbing Hephaestion's hardness between them.

Hephaestion groaned and gripped Alexander's shoulders, pulling him down harder on his lap. Alexander couldn't help it, the way Hephaestion was moaning went directly to his dick and pretty soon they were panting and thrusting, chasing release.

Alexander, remembering what Hephaestion had done the first night they were together, reached his hand between them grasping both of them in his fist.

"Alexander..." Hephaestion moaned, nipping at his ear.

Alexander began stroking them, and while he may have intended to start out slowly, it very quickly devolved into desperate movements as they fucked into his fist. Hephaestion came first, his cock pulsing as he spilled into the bath, but Alexander followed soon after; the noises Hephaestion was making were too much for him not to.

For quite some time, they just sat there, holding each other. Hephaestion ran his fingers through Alexander's wet, blonde hair and held him close.

"I'm glad I'm not just a number," Alexander whispered.

Hephaestion didn't respond, but kissed Alexander sweetly, holding him close. They sat that way for quite some time, until the water had gotten cold and Alexander could hear the preparations for the naming happening outside. They exchanged loving touches as they dressed, a squeeze here, a caress there and

CHAPTER SEVEN

Alexander began to think that he genuinely couldn't remember what his life had been like before this.

Just as they finished getting ready, they heard a knock on the door.

"Enter," Alexander called.

Thetima pushed the door open and smiled softly upon seeing the sweet scene inside. "Oh good, you're ready." Thetima turned and gestured for several other servants to enter the room. They were carrying a variety of chests, some large and some small. Alexander recognized them; he realized they were his father's royal robes and jewels.

Over the years, his father had accumulated a variety of expensive and extravagant attire from his many conquests. Whenever he got back from one of his expeditions, he would always have his servants sort through the riches gathered and set aside the finest things for himself. After this, he had the rest of the loot sent to the treasury so he could gift it as presents and favors to the noblemen and women of his kingdom, as well as visiting dignitaries.

Alexander stepped back and watched as several of the servants placed the largest of the trunks on his chamber floor and opened it, revealing robes of rich and varying colors.

"You should wear the green one," Hephaestion whispered over his shoulder, sending a chill down Alexander's spine. "I've always thought you look incredible in green."

Alexander blushed as he heard Thetima speak up from behind them, "He's right, you know."

Alexander let Thetima and Hephaestion doll him up in the robes and jewelry, yaying and naying the accessories as they went through them. Finally, they settled on golden cuffs and a collar adorned in jewels that sat on his shoulders, across his chest and back.

"You don't think this is too much?" Alexander asked, adjusting under the weight of the gold. "It feels like a lot."

"It is a lot," Thetima responded, straightening Alexander's robe. "But it's supposed to be. This will be the first time the subjects will be seeing you being presented as their king. It is important that you give off a Kingly air."

Alexander nodded and swallowed nervously. Hephaestion and Thetima led him out of his chambers and down the hall toward the balcony where he would be presented.

"Wait here and try not to pass out," Hephaestion teased. Alexander frowned at him, but took a few deep breaths for good measure. He hadn't thought that this day would come as soon as it had, but he had been trained his whole life for this and instincts eventually took over. He tightened his abs and drew back his shoulders, preparing his stance the way he'd been taught. Keep your head high, chest out, and eyes above the heads of others in the crowd.

You are a King.

Never let them forget it.

One of the members of the guard nodded at him and he stepped forward through the curtains and onto the balcony to greet his kingdom.

8

Chapter Eight

"Do you think so?" Alexander joked, leaning in towards Hephaestion.

"I do," Hephaestion replied, intertwining his fingers with Alexander's. Alexander laughed, bumping shoulders with Hephaestion and popping another grape into his mouth. "Just listen: your father conquered as much as he did alone and that was incredible. But, you were trained by him to be better than he ever was and you're not alone."

Alexander rolled onto his back, looking up at the top of the tent. He let his head fall to the side so he could see Hephaestion. Ever since he'd become king, they'd been inseparable. The servants had even stopped packing separate lodging for Hephaestion whenever they'd leave the city.

The first couple of times they did, it ended up going unused, and the men began getting used to seeing Hephaestion retire to the king's tent at the end of the night. This time, they were on their way to Troy for a royal banquet. Alexander much preferred the fighting part of building an empire, but he had grown used to the diplomacy that was required of him as king. As long as Hephaestion was by his side, he truly felt like he could take on the world.

"Hey, Hephaestion." Alexander scooted closer to the black-haired man and Hephaestion vocalized his acknowledgment. "What do you know about Troy?"

Hephaestion lifted an eyebrow and sighed. "Not a whole lot. That's why we are going, isn't it? To get more insight about the area?"

Alexander shrugged. "I guess. I just don't remember learning a whole lot about it."

"Well," Hephaestion began, a sly look on his face, "there is one thing I remember."

"What's that?"

"Do you remember the legend of Achilles?" Alexander looked up in recollection.

"Ah, yes." Alexander nodded. "My supposed brother by Zeus?"

"The very same." Hephaestion grinned wider. "You remember how he had his loyal friend and companion Patrocolus?"

Alexander nodded again.

"Well," Hephaestion continued looking rather proud of himself, "I heard Aristotle talking about a theory that the two were lovers."

Alexander propped himself up on his elbows in interest. "Achilles and Patrocolus?"

"Mhm," Hephaestion affirmed. "They were lovers, and according to legend, they were together until the day they died."

Alexander tilted his head and thought about the implication of this. "Didn't Achilles eventually take a wife though?"

"He did." Hephaestion nodded. "But, despite his marriage, he never let anything stand in the way of his potential happiness."

Alexander smiled and threaded their fingers together again. "Is this you trying to make me feel better about the fact that my mother, and most of the kingdom, is demanding I take a wife?"

Hephaestion feigned offense. "What? Can't I just tell you a story?"

"I suppose you can." Alexander leaned in and pressed his lips to Hephaestion's in a kiss.

For the past few months, Olympia had been 'stealthily' inserting women of influence into his circle. First, she was the daughter of a local noble. His mother had brought her to dinner

CHAPTER EIGHT 93

under the guise of taking her in as a companion. Alexander had believed her at first, happy that his mother was still making friends and keeping herself busy. However, when she showed up at dinner the next day and the day after that... and the day after that, Alexander began to doubt his mother's intentions.

On top of all that, the visiting woman did not seem to be aware of the nature of Hephaestion and Alexander's relationship. One night after dinner, Olympia had pulled Hephaestion away to assist with something of utmost importance and the woman had asked Alexander to walk with her around the gardens.

Alexander hadn't seen any reason not to so he agreed. It had started out tame enough, he listened as she spoke about her interest in the theater and he'd even shared with her one of his favorite books he was reading. He was so invested in the conversation that he had not noticed that she was slowly leading him back to his chambers.

When they reached the doors, she had leaned in to kiss him, receiving nothing but a hand to the shoulder and a "What are you doing?"

She had pitched her case like a professional, batting her eyelashes and pressing her ample bosom to his chest. Unfortunately for her, Alexander had a much... different taste.

He was in the process of turning her down when Hephaestion came around the corner, having escaped from whatever his mother had demanded his assistance in. One panicked look from Alexander had Hephaestion swooping in to his rescue, peeling her hands off of him and making some excuse about needing to retire.

She almost followed but stopped dead in her tracks when Hephaestion looked back and smacked Alexander's ass, making direct eye contact with the poor girl. Hephaestion had thought it was hilarious, Alexander had chided his mother the next day for deceiving him, but neither of them would ever forget the look on that poor girl's face as Hephaestion kissed Alexander with tongue as the door closed.

Alexander hoped that his mother would get the message after that, but unfortunately she did continue to try. Though, since her previous ruse had been seen through, she needed to get craftier about her actions.

Once she "accidentally" ran into Alexander when he was making his way over to the stables from a delegate meeting. This time he had the foresight to question what she was doing all the way out by the stables. She'd explained it away by stating that she was simply receiving an old friend who was visiting and had just arrived. He relaxed a little until he saw a woman, half his mother's age, that he'd never seen before in his entire life come around the corner. His mother suggested that Alexander should show her around while she retired as she was getting a terrible headache.

CHAPTER EIGHT

Luckily for Alexander, his mother had neglected to check if he had anything else planned for the day and as it turned out, he was, in fact, busy.

Another time, his mother employed a local woman to "tutor" him in the ways of pottery making. That ended when Alexander showed up to have his tutor try to suck him off in the hallway on the way to their lessons.

The most recent and frankly embarrassing attempt happened three days before they left for Troy. Alexander had come back to his chambers after a long day of training, muddy and sore, ready for a hot bath. But when he opened the door to his chambers, he was greeted with four naked women laying on his bed provocatively.

On a typical day he would have stormed through the palace and yelled at his mother but today he was just too damn tired. So instead, he just closed the door again and made his way to Hephaestion's chambers to bathe, intercepting Hephaestion on his way to meet him.

Hephaestion had asked what was going on, as they rarely slept anywhere other than Alexander's Kingly chambers, but Alexander had just shook his head and remained silent. After bathing and getting into bed, Alexander explained what had happened but after that moment, they never spoke of it again.

Frankly, he was excited to get out of the palace and remove his mother from her element. He would have preferred to put some distance between them but despite never having any interest in out of town trips before, upon hearing that they were heading to a party; no doubt filled to the brim with eligible bachelorettes, Olympia had insisted upon coming.

They only had one leg of the journey left remaining so all too soon, Alexander knew that he would be surrounded by fawning noblewomen and daughters of dignitaries. As they entered Troy, they were welcomed by a lineup of Troy's finest warriors, saluting them on either side of the road. The walls of Troy were just as beautiful and impressive as Alexander had heard in legend and seeing them in person was truly a sight to behold. The city square was bustling with life, evidently their arrival had caused quite a stir and there was a sea of people gathering around to greet the visitors.

"They really outdid themselves, didn't they?" Hephaestion whispered over to Alexander as they rode through the cobblestone streets. Alexander nodded, they truly had.

It wasn't uncommon for cities and palaces to decorate for parties they were throwing, but Troy had taken it one step above and adorned the entire city in colorful flags, tapestries, and women in costumes handing out colorful necklaces and drinks. The road up to the palace was lined with candles that glowed gently in the dusk, leading up to the palace which was surrounded in the light of the setting sun.

CHAPTER EIGHT 97

"Why are they throwing this party again?" Hephaestion inquired, turning and smiling at some children who had made their way to the front of the crowd to see the horses.

"I guess there are several noblewomen coming of marrying age," Alexander replied. "They probably just wanted an excuse to show them off to as many powerful men as they could."

"Especially you." Hephaestion grinned, teasingly.

Alexander rolled his eyes. "Yes, one thing that I absolutely hate about being King and expanding the empire. Everyone seems to want a piece of it."

Hephaestion laughed out loud, throwing his head back.

"Sometimes I wish that everyone would just leave us alone," Alexander mumbled under his breath.

As they entered the palace, they were received by the King himself, Priam.

"Ah. Alexander." The old man grinned through his beard.

"Priam," Alexander reached out an arm, grasping the other King's forearm in welcome. "It's been far too long."

Priam nodded and turned, indicating for them to follow. Alexander fell in step with Priam, Hephaestion slightly behind him to his left. "I believe the last time I saw you, you were a mere child." Alexander nodded in acknowledgment. "I am terribly sorry to hear about your father, though. He was a great man."

Alexander smiled softly at the old man, "Thank you. We received your gifts shortly after the funeral, they were beautiful."

Priam pursed his lips in thought. "Yes. I'd hoped you would enjoy them."

Priam led them into the palace, down one of the long hallways, and into the library. He waved his hand dismissing the guard as they took a seat. "So, Alexander." Priam began. "I believe you know one of the reasons I have requested that you come tonight."

"I assumed it had something to do with the fact that several noblewomen in this city are becoming of marrying age, is it not?" Alexander spoke plainly. Priam was one of the few people who'd known him for most of his life, so despite this being a meeting among Kings, it was also a meeting of old friends.

"Yes." Priam affirmed. "But specifically, there is a Bactrian nobleman bringing his daughter."

"Bactrian?" Hephaestion raised an eyebrow.

"Yes." Priam nodded. "For years we have had some tension with the kingdoms to the East and over the years we have brokered some, advantageous marriages between members of our upper class. However, unfortunately, it has not been quite enough to ensure a positive relationship between our societies."

Alexander nodded.

"I am far too old to take a new wife, marrying into an alliance with the Persians or Bactrians does nothing if I die too soon. So..."

Alexander clenched his jaw, he now understood where this was going.

"I would like you to consider taking her as your wife, Alexander."

Alexander was silent for a few moments, thoughts buzzing around in his head, when he felt Hephaestion's warm hand on his arm. Alexander glanced over and locked eyes with Hephaestion, taking comfort in him being here. "I am not looking for a wife," Alexander replied.

"I am far too busy with the expansion of the empire to take one and I do not believe that it would be a good move."

Priam nodded slowly, eyeing Hephaestion's hand on Alexander's arm. Taking notice of the suspicious glance, Hephaestion pulled his hand away and cleared his throat, sitting up straight.

"I see." Priam placed his fingertips together. "Perhaps a member of your court then?" He asked, gesturing to Hephaestion.

"No," Alexander said far too quickly. "I mean..."

"Alexander." Priam snapped him back to the moment. "I have heard from your mother Olympia that you had no interest in taking a wife, but I believed that it was likely due to the fact that there had been no appropriate matches for you yet, however, I now see that this is not the case."

Priam stood, signaling Alexander and Hephaestion to stand as well. "There are Kings who take wives later in life, true. However, in the interim, they will typically have several consorts who live with them and..." Priam cleared his throat. "Attend to their needs."

Alexander suppressed a blush and tried not to think about how Hephaestion had been choking on his cock not the night before.

"My suggestion," Priam continued, "would be to at least speak to her father and explain that you are not looking for a wife right now, but to imply that you would be open to marriage later down the line to solidify your alliance. Right now the Persians are not a problem, but they very well could be, and if they manage to take us down, they will be coming for you next."

"That is very wise King Priam." Hephaestion spoke up, Alexander felt as though his mouth was full of cotton.

"And Alexander..." Priam continued, heading towards the door. "Even if you are not to marry right now, I highly suggest that you take a woman. Lest people begin to talk."

"Yes... thank you." Alexander got out, nodding slowly. With that, Priam left the two of them in the library, still digesting the old King's advice.

They stood in silence for a moment, neither daring to say anything. Alexander took a deep breath and turned to his lover, panic in his eyes.

"Okay." Hephaestion reached down, taking Alexander's hand in his. "Let's just talk to them tonight, the nobleman, his daughter, and anyone else who happens to be there."

Alexander nodded numbly.

"We will figure something out. Alexander." Hephaestion took Alexander's face in his hands. "We will. I promise."

Hephaestion leaned down and kissed Alexander, cradling his face as if he were the most precious thing on earth.

"Come on, let's go get ready."

9

CHAPTER NINE

The evening came far too quickly for Alexander's taste. Fully understanding why he was here put a real damper on everything. He'd hoped that he would at least be able to have some fun with Hephaestion tonight, but from the sound of Priam's advice, that would not be advisable. He would be expected to mingle, look at all the women and rate them like this year's harvest and determine if any of them were worth his time.

He couldn't even imagine being born as a woman, though given his preferences, it might have made his life simpler.

The guards walked him through the corridors leading into the ballroom. Hephaestion had gone earlier with the other members of his court to avoid suspicion and while it had made sense, Alexander was extremely unhappy about it. As he stood outside the door, he heard trumpets sound and a distinctly male voice announce his presence. When the doors flung open, Alexander searched the crowd for Hephaestion, finding him standing to the side of the room, in the front row of the spectators.

He smiled softly and gave Alexander a reassuring nod and Alexander immediately felt the anxiety drain out of his chest; that's right, he wasn't doing this alone. Hephaestion was here, Hephaestion would always be here, they would figure this out.

He let his eyes wander over Hephaestion's chiseled features and broad shoulders. He was beautiful, he was comforting, he was home...

Alexander loved him...

Oh.

Alexander felt a blush creep up his face at the thought. In the back of his head, he heard the announcer finish speaking and snapped back to reality. He would have to unpack that later, but right now, he had a job to do. The music started and a lovely woman approached him, asking him to dance. He nodded and took her arm.

The next few songs were a blur of women in beautiful gowns, dignitaries approaching him to talk shop, and guards checking in with him to ensure he was safe. It was a lot and Alexander felt as though he might float away, luckily he had someone in the room who knew him better than he knew himself watching out for him.

"Alexander, I haven't had a chance to see you all night." Alexander immediately felt grounded as Hephaestion placed his hand at the small of Alexander's back and spoke into his ear.

"I know," Alexander replied, smiling genuinely for the first time that night. "It's been terrible without you."

Hephaestion grinned slyly and winked. "I know the feeling."

"King Alexander." The two men turned around as they heard Alexander's name called out by a voice they did not recognize. Upon turning, they were greeted by a Bactrian man adorned in lavish robes and jewels and trailing behind him was a lovely dark skinned woman with long black hair. Alexander mused that she looked similar to what he'd imagined Hephaestion would look like had he been born a woman.

Alexander reacted almost a second too late, smiling. "Oxyartes. What a pleasure to meet you, I heard that you were going to be in attendance tonight."

Oxyartes reached out a hand and shook Alexander's in greeting. "Yes. When I heard that you were going to be coming tonight, I simply had to." Oxyartes stepped to the side, indicating for the young woman by his side to step forward. "This is my daughter, Roxana."

Alexander nodded his head in acknowledgment as the young woman bowed deeply. "King Alexander, it is an honor to meet you."

"Likewise," Alexander replied. He glanced to the side, saw King Priam staring along with a few of the other nobles from the area, and remembered what he was meant to be doing. "Um, Roxana. Could I possibly convince you to join me for a dance?"

Roxana's eyes lit up and she curtsied deeply again. "I would be honored." Her father was watching over the two of them like the proudest parent in existence. He even exchanged glanced with a couple of other Bactrian and Persian nobles almost as if to say, 'See? I told you she would pique his interest.'

Alexander put on his most convincing smile and extended his arm for Roxana to take. His heart began to pound as they made their way to the dance floor and not in a good way. Even so, he knew what he was expected to do, so he took Roxana by the hand and waist as he'd been taught for so many years, and paraded her around the ballroom. He felt extremely lucky that he was not required to look at his partner for these types of dances, he didn't think he could stand to see her excited face.

Once the song was finished, the couple made their way back to Roxana's father and Hephaestion who had been standing and watching. Oxyartes bowed as Alexander walked back up to them, completely ignoring his daughter. Alexander felt a twinge of guilt, he truly hated how obvious it was that her father was simply using her for an advantageous marriage.

"Hephaestion was telling me that you are not at the current moment, looking for a wife." Alexander glanced gratefully over to the taller man. Hephaestion simply nodded and continued in his explanation.

"We are extraordinarily busy as I'm sure you know, but of course, we would be more than happy to revisit this in the next couple of years." Oxyartes perked back up at this, looking over at Alexander for confirmation.

"Ah, yes." Alexander nodded as convincingly as he could while simultaneously feeling a little sick to his stomach about the whole situation. "Roxana." He turned his attention to the woman he'd danced with who was standing behind her father now, playing with her fingers nervously. "As Hephaestion has explained to your father, I am not looking for a wife at the moment. However," He took one of her hands in his and kissed her knuckles. "I can promise you that I will take no other wife until we revisit this conversation."

Roxana lit up at this promise and nodded. "I understand King Alexander. Thank you for your consideration."

Alexander felt that ping of guilt again radiating throughout his body. "If you all will excuse me," Alexander addressed the group. "I am going to get some air, I will be back."

Hephaestion moved to follow, but Alexander put his hand up and shook his head. The last thing he needed were more rumors immediately after he'd turned down a marriage offer. Alexander turned and made his way out into the garden.

Once he reached an acceptable distance from the venue, Alexander let himself stop and drop the facade for a moment. He clenched his hands into balls and swallowed, feeling tears gather at the corners of his eyes. Not only could he not love a woman in that way, but now he was also actively lying to innocent people who had no ill intent towards him. Alexander looked up at the sky and pinched the bridge of his nose. He felt his body wracked with waves of nausea and was just about to head back inside to inform everyone that he was about to retire early when he heard muffled voices coming from the other side of the garden.

"Get in there Barsine."

"Why? So you can whore me out to rich nobles and let them rate me like a farm animal going to the slaughter?"

"This is not a discussion, Barsine. You will get inside now or..."

"Or what father? Or what?"

Alexander knew that this conversation was not for his ears but it had distracted him from the panic he was experiencing and he couldn't help himself. He walked silently toward the voices until he was standing next to a statue, concealed by foliage. Around the corner was what looked like a Persian noble and who seemed to be his daughter.

"I did as you said already! I married Memnon and it almost killed me!" Barsine whisper-shouted at the older man.

Barsine's father grabbed her arm. "Yes well, now that he's dead, you need to find another husband."

Barsine snatched her arm away, stumbling back a couple of paces. "No. I will not let another man violate me in that way."

Alexander lifted his eyebrows.

"Barsine, it is not a violation, it is a wifely duty." Barsine physically recoiled as her father reached out to her again. "You need to get in there, I'm doing this because I care about you."

"Bullshit." Barsine spat. "If you really cared about me you wouldn't have sent Farah away."

Anger crossed her father's face. "This again? I know you think you loved her, but it would have simply gotten in the way of you being a wife."

"Fuck you." Barsine retorted, pain contorting her face. "Just leave me alone."

Barsine's father threw his hands in the air and stormed out of the garden, passing Alexander in his hiding spot and headed back towards the palace. Alexander turned back to see Barsine sit heavily down onto a bench and bury her face in her hands.

Alexander wasn't sure why he did it, it could have been because she was feeling the same way he had been moments before, or perhaps because her father had mentioned a female lover, but either way, Alexander stepped out of the bush and walked over to where the woman was sitting, placing himself next to her on the bench.

"I thought I told you to go the fuck awa..." Barsine began, sounding tired and broken but stopping in her tracks as she looked up to see someone who was certainly not her father. "I... you... you're King Alexander."

Alexander saw several emotions flash over Barsine's face before she started to scramble to her feet. Alexander shook his head and gently wrapped his hand around her wrist. "Please don't. My entire night has been people fawning over me and I... that's not why I came over."

Quickly Alexander's mind flashed back to her father grabbing her and he looked down to see his own hand around her wrist. Alexander let her go as if she'd burned him. "Ah, I'm sorry... I didn't... I should have asked."

Barsine was frozen for several seconds in her half up/half down stance before she seemed to make up her mind and sat down warily next to Alexander. "So, why?"

Alexander lifted his head and turned to look at her. She was very pretty, with long brown hair that tumbled down her shoulders in tight curls. Freckles dotted her face and her eyes were lighter than most darker skinned people he'd met, but they seemed to suit her. "What?" Alexander asked.

"If that's not why you came over, why did you?" Barsine asked softly.

Alexander blinked a couple of times, not really sure of the answer himself. Alexander shrugged, "I was taking a walk and I heard you and your father arguing."

One of Barsine's eyebrows lifted, "So you came over to apologize for eavesdropping?"

Alexander barked a laugh, it had been such a long time since anyone had spoken to him that way aside from Hephaestion. "Sure." Alexander sighed and settled into his seat on the bench. "I apologize for eavesdropping, that conversation was very clearly not for my ears, but I did not walk away."

Alexander glanced at the woman at his side, her face was a mixture between disbelief and amusement. "Well." Barsine leaned back onto her palms, relaxing a little. "I suppose I can forgive you, since you're the King of Macedon and all."

Alexander chuckled. "How kind of you."

They sat in silence for a few minutes, just feeling the gentle breeze moving through the garden and looking up at the stars.

"My father wants me to get married again." Barsine broke the silence.

"I heard." Alexander kept his gaze at the sky, he didn't want to overwhelm her. She clearly needed someone to talk to and he didn't want to back her into a corner by staring.

"I won't do it," Barsine said softly.

"Why should you?" Alexander shrugged, letting his gaze slip to the side slightly.

Barsine pursed her lips and took a deep breath. "Because he is my father and he tells me I must. But..." Alexander waited patiently for her to continue. "If I marry someone, I will have to sleep with them."

Alexander nodded. "And you don't want to?"

"I can't." Barsine got out in a choked voice. "The idea of sleeping with a man... it makes me sick to my stomach. With Memnon, we only did it twice, and I was so relieved when he died, which is terrible of me but... I was free, I'd never have to suffer him entering me and panting on top of me ever again."

Alexander turned his head so he was looking over at Barsine. She seemed to physically shrink at the memory, curling in upon herself. "What will happen to you after tonight?"

Barsine grimaced and pulled her knees into her chest. "My father will likely arrange a marriage for me and I will be forced to comply. Then, if I do not bear a child for that man, and they die, I will have to begin the cycle again."

Alexander nodded thoughtfully before he inhaled as an idea struck him.

"Barsine." He said, turning to face her on the bench. She turned, leaning back slightly.

"What?"

"You do not want to get married again."

"Right."

"And you do not want to sleep with another man."

"Yes, but what..."

"Stay with me here..." Alexander interrupted. "And if you do not, your father will choose for you, correct?"

Barsine blinked a couple of times before nodding.

"Come back to my chambers with me tonight." Barsine frowned and opened her mouth to protest but Alexander put his hand up. "We won't do anything, we will just make everyone think we did. Then, if you would like, you can come with me at my palace as 'my lover." Alexander used air quotations for the last two words. "This way, you won't have to get married or do anything you don't want to do, but your father will still get what he wants. I'm pretty sure that being the concubine of a King is better in his eyes than being the wife of a random noble."

Alexander stopped and waited for Barsine to respond but she stared at him like he was crazy.

"Please say something." Alexander pleaded, suddenly feeling very self-conscious about proposing this to a woman he had just met.

"You're insane." Barsine got out, before laughing and shaking her head.

"Yes..." Barsine looked at Alexander with a bewildered expression on her face. "But... why? Why would you do that?"

Alexander snorted, in absolute disbelief of his luck. "Because Barsine, I believe that we have very similar problems and I think we can help each other."

Barsine opened and closed her mouth a couple of times before understanding sparked in her face. "So... the rumors..."

"Yes, they're true," Alexander confirmed. "But if we are seen together tonight on our way to my chambers I believe that will do the trick."

Barsine's eyes were as wide as saucers and she began to smile. "Really? Like this isn't a joke? You'll just let me come live with you as what?"

"Friends." Alexander shrugged. "We'd have to spend time together to keep the rumors alive but outside of that, you would be free to live your life however you see fit."

Barsine was speechless, considering the option Alexander had laid out for her. After a couple of moments, she pursed her lips together resolutely and nodded. "Yes, okay, let's do it!"

Alexander grinned and stood up, offering his hand to the woman. She immediately took it and stood up next to him. Alexander took off in a run, holding Barsine's hand, through the garden. He was smiling so much, his cheeks hurt.

As they passed the palace, a couple of noblemen, including Barsine's father and Hephaestion were standing out on the terrace. Alexander waved and called out. "Apologies for the rudeness, but Barsine and I will be retiring to my chambers for the evening."

Barsine giggled and kept running past the shocked faces with her new "lover". They passed several more people on their way back to Alexander's chambers including King Priam, who looked on approvingly.

Once they reached the room, Alexander slammed the doors shut and they both collapsed on the bed, laughing and catching their breaths. Barsine flipped over onto her stomach and met gazes with Alexander.

"Is this insane?" She asked between giggles.

"Absolutely." Alexander replied, "But it just might work."

CHAPTER NINE

They devolved into giggles again before finally getting themselves together, sitting cross-legged on the bed, facing each other.

"So," Alexander began, "What do you really want to do?"

Barsine sat thoughtfully for a moment, "Well, if we want them to believe us, we should probably make some noises and jump around."

Alexander took a pillow and threw it at his new friend, earning another laugh. "That sounds awfully embarrassing."

"Yes." Barsine admitted, placing the pillow on her lap. "But the less we leave up to their imagination the better."

Alexander nodded, "That's fair."

Barsine took a deep breath and smiled nervously before letting out an absolutely filthy moan. Alexander slapped a hand to his mouth, trying desperately to stifle his laughter. Barsine buried her face in the pillow on her lap, shoulders shaking with giggles. After a couple of seconds, she sat up and mouthed "your turn".

"What noises would I even make?" Alexander whispered, chuckling. Barsine did not give him an answer but instead leaned forward and twisted Alexander's nipple, eliciting a surprised yelp. Barsine dissolved into quiet laughter again, tears streaming down her face.

"That was incredibly, not sexy." She whispered between breaths.

Alexander frowned at her playfully before grabbing her by the waist and flipping her over, pulling out a surprised "ahh!"

Barsine lightheartedly slapped him on the chest, still laughing. "Knock it off, your highness. They're going to think that you're into some incredibly weird shit."

Alexander made his way to the headboard and replied, "Let them think whatever they want." Barsine raised an eyebrow as she watched. Alexander worked his way to his knees and began to shake the headboard rhythmically, bouncing as he went. "Oh, Barsine!" He cried, slapping his hand to his mouth to stifle his laughter.

Understanding what he was doing, Barsine got to her knees as well, smacking her own ass loudly, "Alexander... ahhh! Yes."

After a while Barsine looked over to the door and then back to Alexander whispering, "We've been at this for quite some time, should we finish soon?"

Alexander bit his lip to stop himself from bursting into laughter again and nodded. He grunted convincingly and stopped the banging of the headboard. Barsine cried out again indicating her own climax and they both stopped bouncing, afraid to move, smiling like madmen. After a couple of moments, they heard several pairs of footsteps retreat from the door and finally gave in to another round of quiet chuckling.

"You think that will do it?" Barsine asked, climbing off the bed.

"Oh yeah," Alexander nodded. "I will have one of my guards accompany you to your room tonight and inform your father that you will be joining us for the ride back in the morning."

Alexander got up and walked over to the door, but before he could open it, Barsine surprised him by giving him a huge hug. After getting over the initial surprise, Alexander smiled softly and hugged her back.

"Thank you so much," Barsine murmured into Alexander's chest before stepping back and mussing up her hair. She smiled at Alexander's confused look. "Sex hair."

"Ah." Alexander acknowledged. "Smart woman."

Barsine smiled at the compliment. "I believe this will be the beginning of a very wonderful friendship."

Alexander nodded and opened the door. Just outside stood some of Alexander's guard and Hephaestion. Alexander looked over at one of his guardsmen. "Please escort Barsine back to her quarters and help her pack. She will be leaving with us in the morning, and you." He turned to another of his guards. "Please inform Barsine's father of our plans."

The two guards nodded and Barsine stood up on her tiptoes, kissing Alexander on the cheek before turning to leave. "Goodnight my dear."

Alexander snorted and smiled watching her disappear down the hallway. Once they were out of sight, he turned to Hephaestion and immediately his mood dampened. Hephaestion's face was unreadable, pulled tight like he was afraid to show any sort of emotion. Alexander turned to the guards. "You all may go, I need to speak to Hephaestion about our military plans upon our return."

The guards nodded and turned to leave, Hephaestion did not move a muscle, so Alexander grabbed his wrist and pulled him into the bedroom, closing the doors. As soon as the doors were shut, Hephaestion yanked his hand away and backed up, standing several feet away from Alexander.

"What do we need to discuss, sire?" Alexander tilted his head at the sudden formalness.

"Well, I wanted to let you know about my new friend and how she'll be living with us from now on, and I just missed you." Alexander stepped forward, reaching for Hephaestion's face but frowned as Hephaestion stepped away.

"I didn't get to spend any time with you all night." Alexander tried again. "Why are you running from me?"

"Seriously?" Hephaestion's expression broke and hurt flooded his face. "You just finished fucking your new sidepiece and now you want to get cuddly with me?"

Alexander opened his mouth in surprise. "Hephaestion..."

"I mean, I suppose I don't have any real claim on you. I know that Priam suggested you go out and take a woman, but I just never thought you'd go out and do it the very same night and without talking to me first!" Tears began to accumulate at the corners of Hephaestion's eyes. "What happened to not ever being interested in women? Huh? I don't..."

Alexander stepped forward, closing the distance between them and embracing Hephaestion.

"Get off me, Alexander," Hephaestion demanded.

"No." Alexander pulled back, holding Hephaestion by the shoulders. "I didn't sleep with her Hephaestion."

Hephaestion's face changed from hurt to sad confusion. "What? But... I just heard." He turned to look at the door but Alexander took his face in his hands and turned it back to him.

"It wasn't real." Alexander pressed. "Barsine knows about me being... uninterested in women and she has a similar predicament but her father was pushing her to marry again."

Hephaestion's brows knit together in understanding as he began to process everything.

"She is going to come live with us and spend time with me on occasion to keep up appearances but nothing more. Hephaestion, I swear." Alexander searched Hephaestion's eyes for understanding.

"So," Hephaestion began, a tear rolling down his cheek. "You didn't?"

"No." Alexander pulled Hephaestion back into him and this time the larger man did not fight it. "Of course not. I know we've never talked about it explicitly but I don't have any interest in sleeping with anyone else, let alone a woman. But the fact that it convinced even you means that it worked, which means less pressure for me to find a wife."

Alexander held Hephaestion as he began to cry, clutching Alexander's clothes. "I was just so afraid..." He sniffled. "I was afraid that it was all over and that I'd lost you."

Alexander cupped Hephaestion's face and kissed him. "Never, Hephaestion. You'll never lose me. I *love* you."

Hephaestion looked up and locked gazes with Alexander, a ghost of a smile playing at his lips. "Alexander... I love you too, so much... I've loved you for so long."

Hephaestion pulled Alexander in and kissed him deeply. He felt a warmth fill his chest and a giddiness play at the edges of his lips.

I've loved you for so long.

Alexander threaded his fingers through Hephaestion's hair and pulled him in close. "Really?" He asked, sucking at Hephaestion's lower lip.

"Yes, really." Hephaestion smiled into the kiss and stepped forward, stumbling then back towards the bed.

"Wait." Alexander pulled back. "How long?"

Hephaestion blushed and buried his face in Alexander's neck biting and kissing at it pulling a whimper out of Alexander's lips. "Um." Hephaestion mumbled, snaking his hands up the back of Alexander's shirt, holding him by the waist. "Since we were 13?"

"Thirteen?" Alexander balked, pulling Hephaestion back by the shoulders so he could look at his face. Hephaestion was blushing intensely and avoiding Alexander's gaze at all costs. "Hephaestion, look at me." Alexander cupped Hephaestion's face in his hands and chased his gaze with his head. "Baby, look at me."

At the pet name, they both froze, Hephaestion gaze lifted from the floor to Alexander's. "Say that again." The embarrassment had taken a backseat to a much softer look on Hephaestion's face.

Alexander smiled softly. "Baby." Hephaestion absolutely melted, embarrassment forgotten and kissed Alexander again, his tongue playing at Alexander's lips. Alexander allowed himself to be backed up to the bed, sitting down without breaking his lips from Hephaestion's. Hephaestion placed a knee on the mattress between Alexander's thighs, climbing on top of him. The heat of Hephaestion's body hovering over him became too much for Alexander and he found himself pulling Hephaestion's shirt off and throwing it to the side.

He wanted to be closer to him, clothes were just a nuisance getting in the way of Hephaestion's skin on his. He pulled off his own shirt and pushed Hephaestion's hand slowly to the side so their chests would touch. Hephaestion took the hint and shifted his weight onto his elbows, pressing them together. Alexander could feel Hephaestion half-hard against his thigh and rolled his hips up against Hephaestion's quickly hardening length. Hephaestion moaned into Alexander's mouth and migrated his kisses down Alexander's cheek, to his jawline and neck, until he reached a spot right behind Alexander's ear and sucked.

Alexander felt an electric shock of pleasure shoot down his spine, sending blood south at an alarming pace. "Hephaestion." Alexander panted. "I... I need..."

"What do you need?" Hephaestion whispered into his neck. "Anything... I'll give you anything."

"I want you," Alexander begged. "Please..."

Hephaestion nodded and began to sink down but Alexander stopped him.

"No..." Hephaestion raised an eyebrow in question. "I want..." Alexander could feel himself blushing. "I don't even know how it would work but..."

Hephaestion silenced his rambling by pressing his lips to Alexander's, slipping in his tongue. "Are you sure?" Hephaestion's voice trembled as if he was simultaneously both incredibly excited and nervous. Alexander nodded and touched their foreheads together.

"Yes. I trust you... and... I want you." Alexander held Hephaestion's face in his hands. A moment of understanding passed between them and Hephaestion sat up slowly, turning his attention to Alexander's pants. With as much self-control as he could muster, he pulled Alexander's pants off, tossing them to the side. Alexander's breathing was uneven as he was both nervous and incredibly aroused. With great care, Hephaestion lowered himself down, kissing paths down Alexander's chest and abs and down to his thighs.

Alexander's cock twitched as he felt Hephaestion's hot breath between his legs. Hephaestion was proceeding slowly, giving Alexander a chance to say no if he wanted, but Alexander wouldn't. Instead, he just watched, cock dripping with precum as Hephaestion pressed his tongue past the ring of muscle and ate Alexander's ass like it was both his last meal and the most delicious thing he'd ever tasted.

Alexander felt himself getting lost in the feeling when Hephaestion sat back and pressed one finger into Alexander. Hephaestion continued kissing and biting at Alexander's thighs as he got accustomed to the intrusion. This time, however, Hephaestion did not go directly for the sensitive bundle of nerves, instead he inserted a second finger and began stretching. It was a strange feeling but not wholly unpleasant, any discomfort he felt was quickly eclipsed by the feeling of Hephaestion's hand, languidly stroking Alexander's dick.

Alexander threw his arms over his eyes, moaning loudly as Hephaestion pushed his fingers in further.

"Don't do that," Hephaestion said breathily. Alexander felt Hephaestion's hand wrap around his wrist and gently move his arm. His face was flushed and between his legs, Alexander could see his hardness hanging heavily, red and leaking from the tip. "Let me see you."

Alexander blushed but did not replace his arm, shutting his eyes and tilting his head back as he felt Hephaestion push a third finger into him. "Oh fuck." Alexander moaned, pushing back on Hephaestion's fingers, feeling him brush barely over the bundle of nerves that had been so carefully avoided earlier. "Hephaestion... baby... please... I need you."

"Fuck." Hephaestion cursed, trapping Alexander's mouth with his own, Alexander's tongue driving in to meet his. Alexander whined as Hephaestion pulled his fingers out, bemoaning the loss. Hephaestion lined himself up, cock pressing at Alexander's entrance. "You ready?"

Alexander grabbed the back of Hephaestion's neck with both hands and pressed their foreheads together again. "Take me."

Hephaestion's breath hitched and he nodded. Alexander gasped as the head of Hephaestion's cock pushed into him and Hephaestion paused briefly, allowing Alexander to adjust to the new feeling, kissing up and down his neck. After a minute, Alexander whispered to Hephaestion to keep going, so slowly and tantalizingly Hephaestion pushed into him until he was fully sheathed.

"How do you feel?" Hephaestion checked in with Alexander, his hips twitching every now and then, holding himself back in an attempt to give Alexander the time he needed.

Alexander kissed Hephaestion softly. "Full... it feels... good... so good."

Hephaestion groaned softly as Alexander adjusted slightly. "Please move..." Alexander whispered, "I want to watch you come undone."

Hephaestion locked eyes with Alexander and began to thrust slowly at first. Alexander grabbed at Hephaestion's back and kissed his neck, biting at his shoulder. Hephaestion's breathing was picking up and he started moving more quickly finally finding his rhythm.

"Fuck." Hephaestion moaned. "You're so tight... you feel... amazing, Alexander. I love you. I love you..." Hephaestion met Alexander's lips again, winding an arm under the small of Alexander's back tilting his hips slightly. With the next thrust Alexander felt Hephaestion's cock hit the sensitive bundle of nerves head-on and he cried out, Hephaestion swallowing his moans with his kisses. Propping himself up on his free arm, Hephaestion began thrusting into Alexander more and more quickly, hitting his prostate with each thrust.

Alexander felt the heat in his stomach building as Hephaestion fucked into him. "Ahh... Hephaestion... baby... I'm getting close... fuck... it feels so good."

Hephaestion growled and maintained his pace. "Fuck... me too... gods... Alexander..."

Alexander's breath picked up even quicker, reaching his hand down between his legs to stroke himself, tipping over the edge. Alexander inhaled sharply, his mouth open in a silent shout as he came, spilling all over his chest and stomach. Hephaestion swore as Alexander clenched down around him, pushing him over the edge as well. Hephaestion trembled, hips stuttering, Alexander's name on his lips.

10

Chapter Ten

Alexander lay there boneless with Hephaestion on top of him, and still buried inside him. Alexander ran his fingers through Hephaestion's hair, massaging his scalp and holding him close.

He was floating. He couldn't remember the last time he'd been this happy. In fact, he thought, he didn't think he'd ever been this happy.

"Hephaestion," Alexander murmured, kissing the top of Hephaestion's head.

"Hm?" Hephaestion vocalized, clearly enjoying the affection and post-coital cuddling.

"I love you."

Hephaestion moved, his dick slipping out of his hole as he adjusted to the side, pulling Alexander close into his chest. "I love you too. So much, Alexander."

Alexander allowed himself to be held, feeling safe and loved in Hephaestion's arms. He intertwined his legs with Hephaestion's and pulled him closer, eliciting a pleased noise from the taller man. After several minutes of relaxing in each other's arms, Alexander felt something slide out of him and he grimaced.

Hephaestion noticed immediately. "Alexander? Are you alright?"

"Um... yes." Alexander stammered. "But I can feel your cum dripping out of my ass and I feel like we should probably do something about that."

Hephaestion laughed and got up, lifting Alexander in a princess carry. "Yes, we probably should."

Alexander only protested minimally at being manhandled as Hephaestion carried him over to the bath, placing him in the water. Hephaestion climbed in with him and washed them both, taking special care to make sure that Alexander was comfortable. After they were both clean, Alexander slipping his arms around Hephaestion and held him in the warm water.

"Hephaestion." Alexander began. "I know you can't be my wife, but I want you to be the one I come home to every night."

Hephaestion's arms tightened around Alexander at the confession and Alexander blushed, hiding his face in the larger man's chest.

"I would really like that," Hephaestion admitted, kissing the top of Alexander's head. "Alexander? Will you be my partner?"

Alexander tilted his head up and kissed the bottom of Hephaestion's jaw. "Only if you'll be mine."

Hephaestion chuckled. "Deal."

The two dried off and cuddled up into bed. Hephaestion technically had his own chambers arranged for him, but they both had known deep down that he was never going to make it there. Alexander curled up in Hephaestion's arms, kissing him one final time before closing his eyes and drifting off into a deep, peaceful sleep.

The morning came far too quickly for Alexander's taste. It had been a long night and Alexander felt very comfortable and content tangled up in the sheets with his partner. Hephaestion stirred slightly as Alexander stretched.

"Mmm. Morning love." Hephaestion mumbled, kissing Alexander and pulling him in closer to his chest.

Alexander kissed Hephaestion's chest over and over again, still getting accustomed to the fact that he could do that whenever he wanted. "Morning. What is the plan for today? Are we heading out right away or are there more festivities?"

Hephaestion pushed his fingers into Alexander's hair, scratching his scalp. "I believe we are requested at breakfast and then we were going to pack up and head back."

Alexander paused and looked up at Hephaestion. "Should we invite Barsine to breakfast?"

Hephaestion raised an eyebrow.

"I mean, is that something kings do with the subjects of their tantric love affairs?"

Hephaestion laughed and kissed Alexander's forehead. "I don't think so, my love." Hephaestion gave Alexander one more tight hug and moved to get up. "If she's just meant to be a woman in your court, her use is pretty much exclusively dedicated to your sexual desires. Bringing her to breakfast would imply that you like her for something more than her pussy."

Alexander made a face. "But I do like her for more than just her pussy. I don't even like her pussy at all."

"True, but other people don't need to know that. Besides, I think that Roxana will be at the breakfast. Bringing another woman to the breakfast would hardly leave a good impression on the woman that you essentially promised your hand in marriage to in the future." Hephaestion stood and walked over to where his clothes were strewn on the floor the night before.

"I suppose." Alexander swung his legs over the bed and stood up as well, searching for his clothes. "I mean, I guess we will see her the entire ride home. I'm excited for you to meet her Hephaestion, I think you'll really like her."

Hephaestion grinned and handed Alexander his shirt.

"Thank you."

"You're welcome, your highness." Hephaestion teased. "Come on, let's head down to breakfast."

They meandered down to the main hall where some guests had already congregated at their respective tables; among them, Roxana, her father, and the individuals they'd brought with them, Olympia and most of the guards that came with them, and Priam, sitting at the head of the table. His mother pursed her lips when she saw them walk in together and Alexander did his best to stifle an eye roll.

As they sat down, they were greeted by a smiling Roxana. "Hello Hephaestion, King Alexander."

Alexander nodded and smiled over at her as he sat down. He didn't have anything against Roxana, truly, she seemed like a wonderful woman and he was sure that if he were even remotely interested in women that he would be jumping at the opportunity to make her his wife.

"So." Alexander began, watching a servant serve him meat and bread. "Are you enjoying the trip?"

Roxana's face lit up and her eyes flicked to her father, who was looking very smug and proud. "Yes." She replied, her voice was gentle and melodic. "It's quite lovely here and of course, we had a wonderful time at the party last night." She nodded to King Priam and smiled as he grinned and put up a hand.

"That's great to hear." Hephaestion piped up. "So, Roxana, what do you like doing in your free time?"

Roxana smiled, "I primarily enjoy playing the lute and walking through the garden."

Hm... Alexander thought. A generic but pleasant answer; the lute comment was meant to let Alexander know that she was accomplished but walking through the garden was meant to imply that she is a wealthy woman of leisure. It was a good answer, but a boring one. Alexander had met hundreds of women just like her and was not particularly interested. She was reserved and polite, quiet and sweet, nothing like his new friend from last night.

For a moment he paused and thanked the gods for Barsine, had he not run into her, he would have likely been pushed to marry sooner. Fake fucking Barsine bought him some time.

CHAPTER TEN

The rest of the breakfast was fairly uneventful, Alexander went through his kingly talking points, ensuring that he gave everyone an equal amount of attention. Hephaestion, gods bless him, would pick up in the conversation where Alexander ran out of things to say, pulling some of the attention away from him and giving Alexander a chance to actually eat.

After breakfast concluded, the group made their way to the front of the palace where their transportation was waiting. As they exited the palace, Alexander saw some movement in the corner of his eye. Turning, he found himself locking eyes with an irritated looking Barsine and her father. Seeing him step out, Barsine broke out into a huge smile and turned to her father smugly. Barsine's father just stood there for his mouth open for a moment before gathering himself together and leading the group over to meet Alexander.

"When Barsine told me, I didn't believe her." Barsine rolled her eyes and grinned softly at Alexander. Alexander smiled back at her, ignoring her father and extended a hand. Barsine took Alexander's hand and allowed herself to be led over to the carriage, stepping up into the seating area.

"Alexander," Olympia spoke firmly. "What is the meaning of this?"

"Oh, you didn't hear?" Alexander turned nonchalantly, letting go of Barsine's hand. "I have taken a lover."

Olympia's mouth opened and closed a couple of times in shock before she turned to the guards for confirmation.

"Oh, it's true." Hephaestion shrugged. "We all heard them going at it after the party."

The guards, embarrassed to being put on the spot, diverted their eyes but nodded. Olympia shut her mouth and narrowed her eyes. "Oh really?"

"Yes, really mother," Alexander said in the most exasperated tone he could manage. "We met in the gardens last night as I was getting some air. I found her company to be very enjoyable."

Alexander watched as Hephaestion climbed into the carriage as well. "What mother? I thought you'd be pleased."

Olympia frowned but moved towards the carriage, climbing inside. "Thank you for your hospitality, King Priam." Alexander turned, shaking Priam's hand.

"Of course." Priam nodded, looking at Alexander with a knowing smile. Alexander mouthed the words, thank you, and stepped into the carriage himself. Sitting down next to Hephaestion, he watched, amused as his mother began looking Barsine up and down.

"Are you truly my son's lover?" His mother asked skeptically.

CHAPTER TEN 135

"Mother." Alexander chided her. "Is it so hard to believe that maybe I didn't go after the girls you sent me because they weren't my type?"

His mother raised her eyebrows and pursed her lips.

"It's true, Olympia." Barsine nodded, putting on her most convincing "truth telling" face. "Your son here dicked me down so good last night that I couldn't walk this morning."

Hephaestion choked. Olympia stared at Barsine with an expression that was a mix of surprise and repulsion. Alexander covered his mouth with his hand, disguising his shocked laugh as a cough. When Olympia finally recovered herself, she stared at Alexander incredulously.

"What?" Alexander asked innocently as he could. "She's truly one of a kind."

Hephaestion was staring out the window, biting down on his lip hard to keep himself from laughing. Alexander chuckled freely, maybe that would teach his mother to stay out of his sex life.

11

CHAPTER ELEVEN

"I'm not saying it's a bad book, I just think there are better options for your favorite." Barsine pointed out, lounging on the couch in Alexander's room, eating grapes. Alexander was sitting cross-legged on the bed, an offended expression on his face.

"Like what?" Alexander retorted.

"Like the Aeneid." Barsine shot back. "I'm sure you know that the Iliad was influenced by it."

"That's true, but that doesn't make it inherently better." Alexander argued, tossing a grape into Barsine's mouth.

"True but…" Barsine stopped and looked at the door. "Sex?"

Alexander shrugged. "Yeah sure."

Barsine climbed over onto the bed next to Alexander and popped another grape in her mouth. "Oh come on," Alexander complained. "Don't eat while you're fucking me, that's just rude."

"*Sorry*," Barsine replied playfully, putting emphasis on both syllables equally.

"Brat." Alexander teased. "Maybe I will just send you back to your father to get married after all."

"No, no, no." Barsine laughed. "I'm sorry, I'm sorry. Give me that fat cock Alexander."

Alexander rolled his eyes but began bouncing on the bed and making his most convincing sex noises. Barsine quickly joined in, pushing Alexander over and moaning loudly.

In the weeks since they'd returned from the party, they made sure to spend time alone together at least a couple of times a week to stave off suspicion. The implication that Alexander was regularly having sex with Barsine was enough to keep Olympia at bay for now. Alexander had discussed it in depth with Barsine and Hephaestion and had come to the conclusion that his mother just wanted to ensure that the royal line was continued. If he was fucking a woman by his own free will, it meant that he would probably sire a child when he eventually married.

He had of course been correct when he'd said that Hephaestion would like Barsine. The two became fast friends and Hephaestion's initial jealousy became a problem of the past.

The more time they spent with her, the more he was reassured that she truly did not like men in a sexual or romantic way.

However, despite the amount of sex he was supposedly having, he and Hephaestion hadn't gotten a chance to be intimate in the time since they'd gotten back. Alexander wasn't happy about it but it did make sense that Hephaestion would sleep in his own room while they were under such intense scrutiny from Olympia.

Now as Alexander sat at the head of the great table, in a meeting with some of the nobles in the area, he found his mind wandering. Fucking his fist at night just wasn't doing it anymore, he remembered how Hephaestion had worked him open and made love to him like it was as important as breathing. Alexander glanced to the side of the chambers where Hephaestion and some of his guards were standing.

He let his eyes rake up and down Hephaestion's body, thinking about how those hands would feel on him, how Hephaestion's mouth felt wrapped around his cock, how much he wanted to let that man bend him in half and...

Alexander snapped his attention back to the meeting at hand, now was no time to be allowing his thoughts to wander like this. Unfortunately, it was far too late to take back his sinful thoughts. Alexander felt himself hardening between his legs and adjusted in his seat so that his lower half was fully covered by the table. He forced himself to listen attentively as the nobles discussed the financial forecast for the next couple of months; he wasn't truly required here for this meeting, but his presence was ceremonial and as King, it would have been rude to miss it.

He willed himself to listen and focus on the numbers and calculations being thrown around, but it had been too long. Every time he would begin to feel his erection subside, Hephaestion would draw his attention by running a hand through his hair or he would be overtaken by a memory from their night in Troy. It was absolutely hopeless.

So, when the meeting ended, Alexander dismissed the nobles and guards, pretending to be absolutely immersed in the paperwork sitting in front of him. When the door closed he sighed and dropped his head onto the table, his hard-on seemingly mocking him.

"Alexander?" Hephaestion inquired walking over to where Alexander was sitting. "Are you alright? You seemed distracted during the meeting."

As soon as Hephaestion got close, Alexander could smell him, sexy and manly, taunting him. Alexander lifted his head and pulled Hephaestion down by the neck, squishing their lips together desperately. Hephaestion responded immediately, kissing Alexander senseless and winding his fingers through Alexander's hair.

"I have been hard all meeting because I cannot stop thinking about you." Alexander confessed, taking one of Hephaestion's hands and sliding it between his legs to touch his aching erection. As Hephaestion made contact, Alexander's hips twitched and he let out a small gasp. "It's been way too long."

Hephaestion pulled Alexander up out of his seat and pushed him back up against the table so he was sitting on the surface. Alexander wrapped his legs around Hephaestion's torso and pulled him close, exploring Hephaestion's mouth with his tongue. "I have been touching myself every night thinking of you."

Hephaestion groaned and pulled Alexander impossibly close. Alexander could feel Hephaestion's length hardening against him as Alexander rut shamelessly against his lover. "Shit," Hephaestion whispered, his hands exploring the topography of Alexander's body like it was the first time.

"Hephaestion." Alexander pleaded. "If you don't fuck me right now, I think I might actually go insane."

Hephaestion lifted Alexander off the table and placed him on his feet, back to Hephaestion's chest and bent him over the table. "Fuck Alexander, who taught you to talk like that?" Hephaestion groaned.

"You, I think." Alexander retorted a light laugh in his voice, which immediately evaporated as Hephaestion dropped Alexander's pants and began licking at his entrance. Alexander covered his mouth to stifle his moans as he pushed back onto Hephaestion. He had been hard for so long that his cock was already leaking onto the floor.

Hephaestion bit his ass cheek and slid one finger into Alexander, sliding across the highly sensitive bundle of nerves. The sudden intrusion was too much for Alexander to bear and he shuddered, shooting his load onto the floor.

"Did you just?" Hephaestion asked, pausing his minstrations.

"Yes, yes, please keep going," Alexander begged. It felt too good to have Hephaestion inside of him to let him stop now. Hephaestion murmured in understanding and went back to work opening up Alexander's hole. He could feel Hephaestion rubbing himself up against Alexander's hip for relief as a third finger was added. So Alexander reached back and wrapped his hand around Hephaestion's length, stroking it rhythmically. Hephaestion's dick in hand, Alexander felt his own manhood twitch in interest again as it hung between his legs.

"Fuck. Alexander, can I?" Hephaestion groaned, pulling his fingers out.

"Yes, Hephaestion, please. I need you." Alexander begged. Hephaestion cursed and moved to stand behind him, lining himself up with Alexander's hole. Alexander's cock was now fully hard again in anticipation and his cheek was pressed up against the surface of the table. They both moaned as Hephaestion pushed inside. It was easier this time since Alexander knew what to expect, he focused on relaxing to allow Hephaestion to fully sheath himself in one motion. Alexander could see his breath condensing on the glossy surface of the table, his hands clenched in fists above his head.

Hephaestion pulled out halfway and slammed back in, ramming directly into Alexander's bundle of nerves. This time was nothing like their first time, while they had been loving, slow, and careful in Troy, here they were hot, needy, and rough. Hephaestion kept pistoning his hips, his grip bruising, over and over into Alexander's sweet spot.

It was hot and heavy, both of them far too pent up to take things slow. Alexander was feeling so good that he left his hands above his head, ignoring his leaking cock and instead focusing on the full body pleasure he was receiving as Hephaestion fucked into him. Alexander felt himself approaching climax, demanding that Hephaestion go faster, coming untouched again as Hephaestion complied. Alexander heard Hephaestion curse and felt his hips stutter as he clenched around him.

Alexander remained, blissed out and sprawled on the table as he felt Hephaestion pull out and finish on his ass. The pair of them took a moment to catch their breaths until Alexander felt Hephaestion pull him upright and into a kiss.

"Fuck I love you." Hephaestion murmured against Alexander's lips. Alexander smiled and returned the kiss, wrapping his arms around the taller man.

"I love you too."

Once they'd cleaned up as best they could, they left the meeting room, Alexander blushing as they passed two very knowing guards. They practically ran back to Alexander's chambers and fell on top of each other in bed. Alexander sighed and sunk into Hephaestion's embrace; he didn't have anything else planned for the day and was plenty happy to just bask in Hephaestion's presence after having gone such a long time without it.

As they drifted off to sleep, Alexander let himself ruminate on the fact that he'd unknowingly become dependent on Hephaestion's presence in his life. He'd gone so many years without knowing what he was missing and it felt as though his body was demanding that he make up that lost time. He slept well that night in Hephaestion's arms wondering how he could have ever not known how in love with this man he was.

Alexander sat in the war room, fingers massaging his temples. News had arrived from the border scouts earlier that day and Alexander had been rudely awakened to handle the imminent threat of an uprising.

"Who?" Alexander stood from his seat and planted his palms on the table.

"The Tracians and Illyrians have been causing some trouble since your father's death." Regulus spoke matter of factly. "However, we had every reason to believe that they would wear themselves out. Unfortunately, it seems that Thebes has taken it upon itself to rebel and cause further insurrection in the area. My advice would be to march upon the city and address the insurgence immediately before it spreads."

Alexander massaged his temples and took a deep breath. His father had spent the greater part of his life uniting Greece and it seemed like as soon as his father was in the ground, trouble was beginning to stir again. Of course, Alexander also had shared his father's dream for a united Greece and had even considered the possibility of helping his father expand the empire further, however when he'd died, those dreams had gotten pushed to the back-burner. Had this happened any sooner, Alexander wasn't sure that he could have handled it in the way that he needed to, but since it was happening now, Alexander felt as though he could think clearly and consider what needed to be done.

Regulus nodded and bowed his head before departing the table. "While I'm gone, Hephaestion will be my eyes, ears, and hand here in the capital." The others at the table nodded their heads, it made sense that Alexander would put his best friend and battle partner in charge while he was gone. "That will be all." Alexander concluded. "Dismissed."

The council members and guards dispersed and Alexander turned to Hephaestion who'd appeared behind him as soon as the meeting completed.

"Alexander," Hephaestion spoke, a worried line carving its way down the middle of his brow. "I should go with you, not be left behind. You need someone at your side who will have your back."

Alexander placed a hand on Hephaestion's shoulder and softened his gaze. "I would love it if you could come with me," Alexander confessed honestly. "But if there's discontent breeding in the populace, I need someone here who I can trust. My father was assassinated in an attempt for the throne, do you really think that people wouldn't try to pull something like that while I'm away?"

Hephaestion frowned but remained silent.

"You're the only person I trust inherently to keep things in order here while I'm gone." Alexander swept Hephaestion's hair to the side with a brush of his hand. "Okay?"

Hephaestion sighed and took Alexander's hand, bringing it up to his lips. "Okay," Hephaestion murmured. "I don't like it, but you're not wrong."

Alexander smiled softly. "Thank you."

Hephaestion nodded and turned to look at the door. "Well, I suppose we should get you ready to go, shouldn't we?" Alexander nodded and they headed out of the meeting chambers.

It wasn't that long of a trip to travel from Pella to Thebes, but it certainly felt longer without Hephaestion to talk to and pass the time. As the army approached Thebes, horns sounded alerting the city to their arrival. Alexander raised his hand to halt the forward march of the army and Regulus rode up to Alexander's side.

"What have the scouts found?" Alexander asked, keeping his eye on the walls of Thebes for any type of attack.

"The gates are still open, however, I believe that will change now that they are aware of our presence. There are some men who believe the best course of action would be to charge the city and put a stop to the rebellion from the inside."

Alexander frowned. "I'm sure that would be a swift course of action however, that would catch far too many civilians in the crossfire." Regulus nodded at Alexander's observation. "Do we know if it's just the leadership and military in the city that's rebelling or has it trickled down to the commoners?"

Regulus shrugged. "We are not sure. Our scouts were able to get into range to observe the goings on outside of the walls but didn't want to alert Thebes to our presence just yet so they were not able to get too close. However, it doesn't seem that they are

CHAPTER ELEVEN   147

expecting us, so we might be able to begin a siege on the city without giving them time to prepare."

Alexander nodded and considered his options. He was sure that his father would have taken the opportunity to charge right in and get it over with, casualties be damned, but Alexander wasn't sure that he agreed with that approach. Rebellion or not, these were still his people and he didn't want to harm those still loyal to him.

"Give the signal to set up camp," Alexander ordered Regulus. "Then, send a messenger into the city to give the leadership a warning. I'd like to handle this diplomatically if possible."

Regulus nodded curtly and set off towards the troops behind them. Alexander studied the city carefully; this was not his first time leading an army, nor was this his first time leading an army alone. However, it was his first time leading an army that was acting solely upon his will and his will alone. When his father was alive, Alexander had led armies into battle on his orders, following his plan. However, now that he was King, everything that happened was his responsibility and he wanted to ensure that he made the right choices.

Briefly, he regretted leaving Hephaestion in Pella, whenever Alexander needed to make important decisions, he always appreciated being able to have Hephaestion's opinion on his ideas. Hephaestion never held back on his opinion and was an incredible military mind as well as a decent person. Alexander shook off his doubts and turned his horse around to join the troops in setting up camp for the evening.

Camp was completed as the sun began to set, and Alexander had retreated to his tent with Regulus and several other high-ranking generals to discuss siege tactics and had been comparing and contrasting options for the last several hours.

"We could try to take the city through the front gates," Jakov suggested, pointing at the spot on the map indicating the entrance to Thebes. "I understand that your highness does not want to get civilians caught in the crossfire, however, scaling the walls would be more dangerous and utilizing our archers to shoot down guards on the walls could still injure civilians behind it."

Alexander nodded with one hand on his chin, leaning forward and looking at the map.

"Well," Regulus piped in. "We could always..." But he was cut off by a panicked soldier barging into the tent.

"Your highness." The soldier took a knee hastily, dipping his head. "There's a problem."

Alexander was on his feet in a second, throwing on his sword belt as he listened.

"Well out with it son!" Regulus commanded. The soldier looked like he was about to piss his pants but continued with what he needed to say.

"Perdiccas... he - well, he took a regiment of soldiers without orders and decided to ride to the city and take it."

"He *what?*" Alexander couldn't believe this was happening. One of his own generals had gone against his orders and had begun an attack on the city.

"We didn't notice until... well, until the screaming started." Alexander pushed past the soldier and threw open the flaps to his tent. There, in the distance of the city was the telltale smoke rising from beyond the walls.

"Wake up the soldiers and ride to Thebes." Alexander commanded, already moving towards the horses. "Fight the Theben soldiers but spare the citizens, try to keep the damage to the city to a minimum, and if any of you find Perdiccas bring him to me, alive."

The generals scrambled to wake up their regiments and get everyone into fighting formation while Regulus followed Alexander to the horses.

"This will not stand your highness. Perdiccas must be punished for disobeying orders."

"I know." Alexander replied. "But I won't have him dying in his assault and becoming a martyr for his cause. No." Alexander emphasized. "He will face the consequences for his actions in Pella, for everyone to see."

By the time they got to the city, it was pandemonium. Residences and shops alike were ablaze and civilians lay dead in the streets, Alexander paused in horror as the exact scenario he was attempting to avoid played out in front of him. Over the next couple of hours, Alexander fought his way into the palace until he had Theban leadership on their knees in front of his sword. In his presence, they were not nearly as bold as they had been with the city walls between them and quickly gave the order for their soldiers to cease fighting. Alexander pressed his middle and forefinger up against the sides of his nose as the leadership was taken away.

"Who is next in line for succession here?" Alexander turned to the court servant who had been attending the leadership. She recoiled in fright as his gaze landed on her and began to shake. A queasiness rolled through Alexander, he did not want to be feared, he wanted to be respected, but the way that this servant was looking at him reflected how he was sure that the rest of the Thebans would look at him from this point on. The thought saddened and disgusted him.

After several attempts to locate the next in succession, a guard finally brought in a boy that could not have been older than 14. Alexander took a deep breath and addressed him as his King.

"We will not hear of this rebellion again," Alexander spoke clearly and with a commanding tone. "Philip may be dead, but there is a new King and I will not stand for this type of treason. We will take the women and children to Pella and Thebes will begin again as a new city under the Macedonian Empire. Do I make myself clear?"

The boy set his jaw as if to convince himself that he was not afraid, and nodded. "Yes, Sire."

"What is your name?" Alexander asked.

"Karanos." The boy replied, his fists balled tightly at his side.

"An apt name." Alexander nodded. "Good for a leader. You will not be as foolish as your parents were, will you, Karanos?"

"No, Sire." Karanos glanced to the side at where his parents were chained and kneeling next to the guards.

"I will not kill them," Alexander spoke, more quietly than before, noting the look of surprise on Karanos's face. "However, they will likely spend their lives in prison for their crimes."

Karanos nodded and swallowed. "That is very kind of you Sire."

Alexander nodded back and turned to retreat from the chambers. "What is the report?" Alexander asked Regulus as he fell into step with Alexander in the hall.

"Six thousand dead," Regulus said, succinct and to the point. Alexander closed his eyes and pursed his lips. "Many of the women raped and the city has been razed."

"Have you located Perdiccas?" Alexander asked, stony faced.

"Yes." Regulus said, gesturing to the courtyard. "He is being chained as we speak, though his men are not taking it very well."

Alexander felt a swell of rage in his chest and set down to the courtyard. He stormed down the steps and into the open space, rain beginning to fall, coming face to face with Perdiccas's men. He stopped just short of one of the men, staring him in the face. "Would you like to join your leader in chains?" Alexander spat.

The soldier shut his mouth but looked over to Perdiccas for instruction. Alexander grabbed his chin and yanked his face back, away from Perdiccas. "Don't look at him. Look at me. Perdiccas will be executed for his crimes in front of all of Pella."

The soldier's eyes widened as he listened. Alexander took a step back and addressed the group of soldiers. "A disgrace, all of you. Traitors." The rain began to pelt the cobblestone and Alexander felt his clothes beginning to soak through, but he did not budge.

"We only did what your father would have done." A voice from the crowd piped up. Alexander stalked over to the soldier who had spoken and drew his sword. He stared daggers into the man's eyes and felt a spike of inconsolable rage as the soldier simply stood there, face calm, as if he was confident that the ghost of Alexander's father would rise up at any moment and pat him on the back for what he'd done.

"Feeling brave against the new King are we?" Alexander asked, drawing back his sword arm. He watched as the man's expression went from smug to sheer terror as he realized his mistake, Philip was dead and would not be intervening. In fact, the gods themselves could fall from the heavens at that very moment and they themselves would not be able to save him from this fate. Alexander brought his sword down, cutting the man down and slicing him from shoulder to hip.

He was sure that he would feel sick about it later, but as the rain streamed down his face, all he could feel was the burning anger in his chest. "Anyone else?" Alexander looked around, holding his arms out in acceptance for anyone else stupid enough to challenge him. These men were laughing at him, they were spitting in the face of everything that he was trying to accomplish and what stung the most was that he knew they were right. His father would have supported their actions in a heartbeat.

The crowd was silent as they watched their comrade bleed out. "Make no mistake." Alexander began, rage dripping from his voice. "There is a new King and while I may not wish violence upon innocent civilians, believe me, that same kindness does not extend to traitors."

The silence was all-encompassing. Perdiccas's men watched Alexander as he wiped his sword on one of the other soldier's pants, leaving the red stains of their brother's blood. Alexander took a breath and sheathed his sword, taking a moment to collect himself, pushing the anger down and addressed the crowd of soldiers with a demeanor dripping with eerie calm.

"This is your one opportunity," Alexander spoke loud and clear. "My father is dead, anyone wishing to continue following him is more than welcome to follow him into the afterlife. I will not tolerate this sort of insubordination in my ranks and we will not be having this conversation again. Do I make myself clear?"

Murmurs spread across the crowd as most of the soldiers nodded in agreement.

"I *said*, do I make myself clear?" Alexander asked again, his voice raised just below a shout. Immediately a resounding "Yes sir!" Sounded in the courtyard. Alexander took one final look over the crowd of men in front of him and turned dismissively.

Immediately Regulus was at his side. "What are your orders, sir?" Together they walked towards the gates as the rain soaked through to their skin.

"We will stay in the camp for the night and leave at first light. We will leave a detachment of men behind to help with the cleanup and ensure that no other issues arise. Leave the traitor outside for the night and ensure that no less than three guards are watching him at all times. He will face his sentencing on our return to Pella."

Regulus nodded and muttered a quick, "Yes sir," before peeling off from Alexander and turning back to address the troops. Alexander made a beeline back to the camp and stormed into his tent, swatting aside the tent flaps on his way inside. Once he was alone in his tent, Alexander let himself pause to think about what had happened that night. First, he felt angry; he clenched his fists and stilled himself to prevent any damage to the tent. He clenched his fists so hard that his forearms shook and the muscles in his hands began to lock up.

Then, he was hit by a profound wave of sadness. He released his grip and took a shuddering breath as he felt tears to begin to prick at the corners of his eyes.

Why did he think that he could do this?

Alexander sat heavily on the bed and turned his hands so his palms were facing the sky. Each hand had four, semicircle shaped cuts that dug into his palm, blood leaking from each one. His brows furrowed as the tears spilled over his eyes and rolled down his cheeks, wracking his body with sobs. Six thousand people, dead, and all because he had lost control of his army.

It was his fault. He knew what his father would have said.

"A good leader will always remain in control of his people. When they fail, it is only because the leader has failed."

Alexander thought of Hephaestion, sitting at home. He would know what to say, he always did; but wasn't that part of the problem? Alexander swallowed and took a deep breath. He depended too heavily on Hephaestion to be a King, he needed to learn to stand on his own and control his kingdom or it was all going to fall apart and there would be nobody to blame but himself.

He stood and stalked over to his bags, kneeling, he rummaged through them until he found a bottle of liquor and some bandages. Alexander set his jaw and uncorked the alcohol with his teeth, wincing as he poured it on his palms. Then he set the alcohol to the side and wrapped each of his hands in a bandage, tucking the end into the wrap once he was finished.

He was not going to allow his reputation as the King to be that of failure and being lesser than his father. He needed to do the one thing his father had tried to do and failed. Alexander thought back to what his father had said to him all those years ago.

"Macedon is too small for you. Once day you will conquer the world."

Alexander laughed sadly to himself, maybe if he did, he could finally step out of his father's shadow.

12

Chapter Twelve

The ride back was solemn. Alexander had instructed the guards to tie up Perdiccas and carry him back tossed over the back of Regulus's horse. It was petty and he knew that he'd gotten his point across the night before and had he just instructed the guards to carry him in one of the carts holding the weaponry it wouldn't have made much of a difference. However, something about the idea of watching Perdiccas walk into the cart to sit comfortably for their ride back rubbed him the wrong way.

Alexander distracted himself with strategy long into the night. In fact, he hadn't truly slept at all. Even now as they rode, Alexander kept turning over the possible routes of expansion in his head again and again. His father had tried to expand the empire outside of Greece but ultimately failed; Alexander would learn from Philip's mistakes and be successful where his father was not. Perhaps then his kingdom would respect and embrace him.

When they arrived back into Pella, Hephaestion was waiting with a few dozen men, ready to receive them. Alexander had sent a messenger back, riding ahead with the information of their victory, but not of the treachery among his men. The last thing he needed was that information getting into the wrong hands and having someone exploit it to overthrow, or worse, kill him. As soon as they got within 50 feet of the palace, Alexander saw Hephaestion's face change from happy and welcoming to concerned.

Of course, he would know something was wrong, Alexander just prayed that it wasn't as evident to anyone else. Upon crossing the threshold to the palace grounds, Alexander turned to Regulus.

"Take the traitor to the prison and set up the square for an execution first thing in the morning." Alexander saw Hephaestion's eyes widen from his periphery but kept his gaze on Regulus. The leader of the guard nodded and rode off in the direction of the prisons, a few men tailing him in the formation. The rest of the men filed in and towards the stables to deposit their horses, but Alexander dismounted, handing the reins to a servant and instructing them to take good care of his horse before heading toward the palace. He heard hurried footsteps behind him but made not effort to slow down as he turned a corner he felt a hand on his wrist.

"Alexander." Hephaestion tugged slightly on his arm, turning him around. "What happened? Are you alright?"

Alexander pursed his lips and set his jaw. "I'm fine. There was some insubordination in the field but the traitor is being taken to the prison and will be executed in the morning." Alexander freed his hand from Hephaestion's grasp and turned again, heading towards his chambers. He sensed that Hephaestion wanted to stop him again, and he was ready for it, but he didn't. Instead, Hephaestion followed him silently to his chambers and closed the door behind them.

Alexander stalked over to his dresser, pulling off his cloak and placing it down as calmly as he could. Hephaestion stood at the door, watching him as he moved around the room, finding things to move, put away, and distract him from Hephaestion's gaze at the door. He hoped that Hephaestion would leave him alone if he continued to ignore him but unfortunately he had no such luck. When Alexander finally stopped, staring at the bracers he'd just taken off, Hephaestion spoke.

"Are you going to tell me what's going on?" Hephaestion asked calmly.

"No," Alexander replied, muscles in his jaw straining. He could feel the sadness at the back of his throat, threatening to overtake him.

"Alright." Hephaestion took a step into the room and away from the door. "Do you want me to leave?"

Alexander opened his mouth to say yes but the word caught in his throat. He remembered how horribly lonely he'd felt alone in his tent after the attack and balled his fists again, gently feeling at the cuts, still fresh in his palms.

"I have to learn how to be a king without you." He said, still staring at the bracers.

"What?" Hephaestion asked. Alexander felt the tears threatening to well in his eyes again and swallowed, holding them back. "Alexander, what happened?"

"Perdiccas attacked Thebes without orders." Alexander got out, biting at his lip to keep back the tears. Hephaestion inhaled sharply but made no move to approach, so Alexander continued. "He and his men did what they said my father would have done and razed the city. 6,000 dead."

"Alexander…" Hephaestion murmured softly, stepping forward.

"Don't." Alexander held his hand up at Hephaestion and he stopped, respecting Alexander's wishes. Alexander wanted nothing more than to run to Hephaestion, wrap him in his arms, let him tell Alexander that everything was going to be alright, and fall asleep. But he knew that he had to stand his ground here.

"I've been a negligent king." Alexander choked out. "I should have been spending more time with the military, expanding the kingdom like my father had. If I have any hope of being the king that he was I…"

"You don't want to be the king he was." Hephaestion interrupted, taking another step towards him. "You said it yourself, your father would have razed that city."

"I razed that city," Alexander shouted exasperatedly, slamming a palm to his chest. "It wasn't my order but because I couldn't control my men, 6,000 were killed, women were raped, and houses were burned to the ground."

Hephaestion watched him with wide eyes as the tears began to fall.

"It was my fault." Alexander sobbed. "My father always had the authority to make decisions by himself but I couldn't. While I sat planning with my generals and seeking council, my men got tired of my waiting and acted on my behalf. I should be able to rule this kingdom with my own choices and not depend on anyone..."

"Your father," Hephaestion shot back. "Was an arrogant fool who made so many mistakes that it got him assassinated."

Alexander shut his mouth without a response to that and Hephaestion stepped closer again.

"You don't need to do this alone. The very fact that you choose to seek counsel instead of making choices based on your every whim just proves how good of a leader you are." Hephaestion's face had softened again. "I, for one, am proud to serve by your side in whatever capacity you'll let me and I know that most of the other generals and noblemen feel the same way. So what if there are one or two people who preferred your father's way of doing things?"

Alexander stood, considering Hephaestion's words. He felt tears rolling down his face and moved to wipe them away, only to find Hephaestion's fingers already there, drying his cheeks. He took Hephaestion's hand in his own and closed his eyes.

"You are an incredible person." Hephaestion cupped his cheek. "And there is no doubt in my mind that you could rule alone, but I also know that would make you miserable. I am here for you, whether you want me here as your friend, partner, lover, confidant, political ally, or any mixture of the above. There is no shame in leaning on people close to you and I never want you to consider that a weakness."

Hephaestion touched his forehead to Alexander's and Alexander could feel the tightness in his chest loosening as he gave in to Hephaestion's comfort.

"You know, I knew you'd calm me down so I had to think rationally about this and that is exactly why I tried to avoid you in the first place." Alexander chuckled.

"I know." Hephaestion grinned and placed a soft kiss to Alexander's lips. "By all means, be upset about what happened, but don't blame yourself for something that wasn't your fault."

Alexander exhaled, the last of the tension leaving his shoulders. "I hate it when you're right." Alexander looked up at Hephaestion and wrapped his arms around his broad shoulders. "I really missed you."

Hephaestion pulled Alexander in by the waist and buried his face in Alexander's neck. "I really missed you too."

"I have to execute a man tomorrow." Alexander mumbled into Hephaestion's shoulder.

"I heard. Do you want me to be there with you?"

Alexander fought his immediate reaction to turn Hephaestion down and stopped to consider what he really wanted. He needed to stand on the stage alone to make his point to the other commanders that he was not to be disobeyed but he also didn't want to completely isolate himself. He knew that he would likely feel like shit the entire time and while having Hephaestion there wouldn't make it okay, he did feel as though it would lend him strength.

"Yes. Please." Alexander replied and he felt Hephaestion's hold tighten.

"I will be directly off to the right in case you need anything." Alexander smiled, Hephaestion had already gathered that he would need to do this alone and was making the effort to be where Alexander needed him to be while still helping him build his new reputation as the king.

"Thank you."

The next morning was a solemn affair, the servants prepared the stage and Alexander donned his ceremonial clothes. He'd made it known among the generals that immediately following the execution they were to congregate in the war room for a meeting; Alexander had something to announce.

He and Hephaestion had stayed up late into the night talking about Alexander's plans to take Persia. Once Alexander had made it clear that he intended to take Hephaestion with him on these escapades, the other man had been on board.

"We'll do it as diplomatically as possible." Alexander had said. "But I don't have any issues using force if necessary."

Hephaestion had agreed, beginning from a diplomatic standpoint, would not only conserve the strength of their armies, but it would also distinguish Alexander from his father, setting the precedent for what his subjects and those serving under him should expect. They hadn't gotten a great deal of sleep, but Alexander was feeling much better about the whole thing as he prepared to step out in front of the crowd.

Which is why, now, as he approached Perdiccas, kneeling on the stage, he did not waver. He gave his statement, addressed the crowd, and swiftly carried out justice. This was his first time executing someone on his own publicly, aside from his fit of rage and despair at Thebes when he'd cut down the soldier. When Philip was king, Alexander would often come to executions and stand by his father's side both to accustom him to what he might need to do as king and to teach him how to handle situations like these.

He held no love for Perdiccas, however, watching the light drain from his eyes gave him no joy. It was unfortunate, but he needed to be made an example of if Alexander had any hope of being a successful military leader. He knew that, and yet, his heart still ached for Perdiccas's family.

After the execution, Perdiccas's body was taken away and the crowd dispersed. Alexander made his way to the side and stepped behind a column so Hephaestion could squeeze his hand reassuringly. Together they walked, side by side to the war room. The rest of the generals trickled in as they made their way back from the execution and took their respective seats. Once everyone had arrived, Alexander spoke.

"I plan to expand the empire into Persia." Other than a few surprised looks, no one seemed to react too strongly. He explained in great detail his plan to leave in several weeks and work his way East. He impressed upon the generals that while it was going to be a military campaign, he was going to try and resolve things diplomatically, the way it should have been attempted in Thebes, and if anyone disagreed, he would happily leave them here.

All in all, the meeting was productive and his generals were a great deal of help in determining logistics. Andeas, one of the older generals, pulled out maps and plans that had been used during his father's rule. Then together with the other generals, Alexander updated the old plans switching certain battle techniques to match his ideals.

Over the next several weeks, the preparations went by quickly. Alexander had told Barsine what was going on and they'd had a very loud goodbye, just for good measure. Behind closed doors though, Barsine hugged Alexander, kissed him on the cheek, and told him to stay safe. Alexander promised her that he would bring new reading material back from Persia.

Before he knew it, the day to depart was upon them and Alexander found himself terrified, but excited as they mounted their horses to set out.

13

Chapter Thirteen

"When do you suppose we will encounter resistance?" Hephaestion asked, riding next to Alexander. The sun had just come up, the company had broken down camp and begun riding immediately. They'd been on the road for over a week now and hadn't encountered any Persian armies. As per Alexander's plan, they had been going about their campaign diplomatically up to this point, every time they would pass a Persian town, one of Alexander's generals would veer off to talk to leadership. Most of the villages and towns they passed were so far removed from any centralized Persian rule that they did not care which kingdom they belonged to as long as they were protected.

There were, however, a couple of places that were difficult and some persuasion had been required. So far, though, there had not been any situations in which they needed to resort to violence.

Alexander pursed his lips to Hephaestion's question. "Ideally, never." Hephaestion chuckled. "But realistically, the further into the Persian empire we get, the more likely it will be that we will encounter an army."

The rhythm of the horses walking had become familiar and even calming to Alexander over the past week. He had forgotten how much he really enjoyed being outside of the city.

"We haven't exactly been quiet about our arrival," Hephaestion noted. "I think it's likely that someone has sent a messenger to the capital by now."

Alexander nodded in agreement and scanned the horizon. Then, his eyes fell onto Hephaestion; Hephaestion and his beautiful raven hair, chiseled jawline, and broad shoulders.

"Are you checking me out?" Hephaestion teased.

"Maybe," Alexander replied laughing a little. "Why? Can I not check out my own partner?"

Hephaestion's lip quirked at that. "Well, when you put it like that." Hephaestion turned his gaze to Alexander and gave him a smile as bright as the sun. Alexander was just about to reply when they heard the horn. It came from their right side and Alexander and Hephaestion locked eyes, their demeanors turning serious. The horn had sounded twice, which meant only one thing, an enemy army had been spotted.

"There's your welcome party Hephaestion." Alexander joked. When they finally arrived at the general who'd made the order to signal them, he gave them an account of what their scouts had discovered. The army had almost 5,000 infantry and 10,000 cavalry and they were situated in a defensible position on the opposite bank of the river. It would be difficult to cross and fight as they would just be waiting on the other side, ready to cut them down.

"Are they interested in negotiating?" Alexander asked.

The general who had called the halt, Cleitus the Black, snorted, "Unlikely."

"Well, I'd still like to try," Alexander replied calmly. The general nodded and rode out to the front where he signaled the Persian army for a parlay. Once they'd responded, Alexander rode out to a shallow area of the river to meet the Persians for conversation.

"We hear you are sweeping the countryside and taking towns and cities in the name of Macedon and we are here to put a stop to it." The Persian general said stoically.

"We are here to expand the empire of Macedon. We are open to negotiation but will not allow anyone to stand in our way." Alexander replied. The Persian general nodded and turned around, riding back towards his army.

"I guess that's a no to negotiation," Hephaestion said lowly.

Alexander shrugged. "I can't blame them, but at least we tried."

Once back among their own men, Alexander spoke with his generals to formulate a plan of attack. Everyone seemed to have a differing opinion but one thing that they could all agree on was that it was highly unlikely that the Persians would cross the river and give up their advantage, so the first strike was theirs to make.

Alexander's second in command, Parmenion, suggested that they wait until nightfall and cross the river, waiting to attack until the next day. But ultimately Alexander decided that if they were going to attack, they needed to do it swiftly and before the Persians could get a chance to create a counterattack. Quickly and with the most care possible, Alexander gathered a small group of cavalry and light infantry, ordering them to cross and draw the army away from the bank.

Alexander watched as the small group took off and turned to Hephaestion. "I need you to lead the infantry across the river; I am going to ride across and buy you some time."

Hephaestion turned his head as if to judge the distance between the banks and then turned back to face Alexander. "Alright, stay safe."

Alexander nodded and placed his hand on Hephaestion's shoulder. "You too."

CHAPTER THIRTEEN 171

Alexander mounted his horse and signaled to the group of men who were to follow him across the river. They sat at the top of the hill and Alexander watched as the small scouting group finished crossing, showering the right side of the formation with arrows. The infantry started in, swinging and hacking through the first line of defense. After that first move had been made, the battle truly began.

Alexander had instructed the squad to slowly pull the forces outwards, breaking their lines. So far, they were doing a decent job, and Alexander saw an opening to begin to reveal itself. With the reflexes of a commander that had been in the military his entire life, he took the opportunity as soon as it presented itself to him.

"Now," Alexander ordered, transitioning his horse into a run. The other cavalrymen followed him down the hill, to the right, and around to the back of the formation. The Persians realized what was happening too late and were poorly prepared to handle the attack from multiple directions at once. Alexander got to work, charging into the formation and heading directly for points of command and places where a change in formation would give the enemy a tactical advantage.

A couple of rows back from him sat a high-ranking Persian official on horseback, mistakenly believing himself to be safe towards the back of the group. Alexander leaned forward into his horse's momentum and drew his sword, with one swift movement, Alexander cut through the chest of the first footsoldier he came across and kept moving. He dodged a spear that was thrown by one of the bodyguards of the official in an attempt to prevent Alexander from reaching them.

Alexander swung his sword again, this time catching a horse in the leg, not turning to watch, but hearing as the horse went down, dropping its rider. The noble's face was becoming more and more concerned the closer he got; then as if realizing that Alexander wasn't going to be stopped, raised his axe, setting his jaw. Alexander swiped again with his blade, cutting down the guards surrounding the nobleman with an expert maneuver of his sword. The nobleman raised his axe and brought it down directly over Alexander's head; Alexander swerved his path slightly and brought his blade down, aiming at the legs of his horse.

Just as Alexander's blade made contact, he heard his horse scream and he was thrown forward, landing heavily on the ground. He'd swerved but not quickly enough, the nobleman's axe had stuck itself in his horse's neck, severing a major artery. Alexander rolled, feeling his shoulder take the brunt of the impact but not hearing anything break. He rolled back onto his feet just in time to see his opponent swinging his axe downward again.

Alexander rolled to the side and swung up with his blade arm, feeling the iron collide with the side of the Persian's armor. The nobleman grunted in pain and dropped his axe arm down, Alexander moved to take another swing when he heard the clang of metal on metal assaulting his ears. Before he could register what had happened, he was falling sideways, a bright ringing filled his ears and the world spun around him as he hit the ground.

Alexander gasped for breath and rolled onto his back. The nobleman had done an upswing with his axe, catching Alexander in the side of the head as he'd dove in to attack. His mind screamed for him to move, to get up, to do anything, but his body was still reeling from the hit. He watched helplessly as the Persian raised the axe over his head once more, ready to bring down the killing blow. He kept his eyes open, not giving his opponent the pleasure of watching him be afraid, steeling his gaze and waiting for the blow.

But it never came. Alexander watched with wide eyes, blood spraying over him as a sword emerged from the nobleman's chest. Blood gathered at the sides of the man's mouth before he was tossed aside off the blade and onto the ground. The world had stopped spinning so much and Alexander grinned as he came face to face with a big, burly man, wearing his colors.

"Your Highness, I think you should probably get off your royal ass and help us out." Alexander grinned and took the massive hand that was extended to him.

"Thank you Cleitus." Alexander managed, as speech was still rather difficult at the moment.

"You took a pretty hefty axe hit to the head just now, you alright?"

"Course," Alexander replied automatically taking a step. Immediately his knees gave out and he felt a strong grip catch him under his arms.

"Perhaps not." Cleitus grunted. Alexander registered himself getting lifted onto a horse and led out of the fighting. From that point; he only registered a couple of things; first, he felt the water of the river on his legs as they crossed back over, second, he heard Regulus barking orders to get him inside one of the tents that had been constructed to tend to the wounded, and lastly, he felt himself being eased down onto a bed. Then, everything went dark.

Alexander woke to the feeling of a damp cloth being dabbed across his forehead. His head was pounding and he desperately wanted to keep his eyes shut.

"Alexander?" Hephaestion's voice found its way into Alexander's consciousness and Alexander took hold of the wrist of his nurse and opened one eye partially to confirm what he already knew. He pulled the hand close to his lips and kissed it.

"That's what they call me." Alexander joked, making the effort to open his other eye. Hephaestion was covered in blood and dirt and had the telltale wrinkles between his eyebrows that appeared when he was worried about something.

"Oh, thank the gods." Hephaestion rested his forehead on Alexander's chest, holding onto his hand. Alexander reached out his other hand and rubbed circles on Hephaestion's back.

"Did we win?" Alexander inquired after a while of sitting in silence.

Hephaestion lifted his head and smiled softly. "Yes, of course, we did. You cut through several of their generals in your rampage."

Alexander smiled and patted Hephaestion on the back. "Good, good. How long was I out?"

"A couple of hours." Hephaestion grimaced and squeezed Alexander's hand tighter. "If I had known that loving you would have made it that much more unbearable when you got hurt, I would have never done it."

"Mmm, you don't mean that," Alexander replied, closing his eyes again.

"No, I don't." Alexander could hear the smile in Hephaestion's voice. "Get some more sleep, you earned it."

Alexander tightened his grip on Hephaestion's hand. "You know what would make me feel better?" Alexander opened his eyes and met Hephaestion's gaze.

"What's that?" Hephaestion rubbed his thumb across Alexander's knuckles.

"If you stayed with me," Alexander replied honestly. Hephaestion blew some air out of his nose in amusement but nodded, climbing into bed with Alexander.

They were both dirty and sweaty from the battle but Alexander didn't care. He felt his body relax as Hephaestion placed an arm underneath Alexander's head and pulled him into his chest, cradling him like the most precious thing in the world. Hephaestion ran his fingers through Alexander's hair and pressed several kisses to the top of his head. Alexander smiled to himself as he drifted off to sleep again, wrapped in Hephaestion's arms.

Chapter Fourteen

The first thing that Alexander realized upon waking up was that he was alone. Instinctively he reached out for Hephaestion but was met with nothing but blankets and an empty cot. He furrowed his brow and then immediately decided against that as he felt a pang of pain in his head. Opening his eyes he did a quick scan of the tent, there were a couple of other beds filled with sleeping patients but otherwise the tent was empty.

Alexander swung his legs over the edge of the bed and sat up slowly. His head hurt but not as much as it had yesterday and for that he was grateful. Carefully, Alexander stood and when it became apparent that he wasn't going to immediately fall over, he made his way out of the tent and into the open.

"Your Highness." Alexander turned to see Parmenion turning the corner. "I was just about to come and check to see if you were awake."

Alexander gestured to himself as he stood. "Have you seen Hephaestion?"

"Yes." Parmenion replied, turning to point. "He's in the commanders' tent, determining the next moves to present to you upon your arrival to the land of the conscious." Parmenion smiled, looking back at Alexander.

"Thank you." Alexander nodded and started off in the direction of the tent. It wasn't that far from where he'd been resting, but the journey took him a little while to make as he kept getting stopped by generals and soldiers to compliment his strategy and how he'd fought. When he finally arrived at the tent, he heard Hephaestion's voice intermingled with a few others. He entered the tent, throwing back the flap, and saw his partner hard at work, sitting in front of a map with Regulus and Cleitus.

"Ah, he's alive." Cleitus was the first to notice him and tilted his head to receive him.

"Yes." Alexander replied, making his way over to the table and taking a seat next to Hephaestion. "So, I hear you all are strategizing. What do you have so far?"

"Well." Regulus shifted in his seat so he could point to the map. "We've come this far. There are several city-states on the way to Gordium, here."

Alexander nodded and waited for Regulus to continue.

"I understand that you are looking to have as bloodless of an expansion as you possibly can and today may have seemed counter intuitive to that, but Cleitus was telling us about a way that we might be able to get back on track."

Alexander raised his brows and turned his attention to Cleitus the Black. "I'd heard about this legend as a child from the merchants who used to visit." He began. "In Gordium there's this knot. Supposedly it was created by this foretold king who rode into the city on an ox-cart in the days of antiquity. Evidently, it's near impossible to get undone."

Alexander waited for Cleitus to continue and when he didn't, he spoke up. "That's great, but what does it have to do with us peacefully taking territory in Asia?"

"Well." Hephaestion interjected from the side. "There's a prophecy that says, whoever unties the Gordian Knot is destined to become ruler of all Asia."

"So," Alexander began tentatively, "you're suggesting we stake our claim on the land by untying an impossible to unravel knot?"

"Yes." Regulus replied this time. All three sets of eyes were on him as he considered the potential of this plan. As weird as it was, a bloodless expansion of the empire would be a lot easier if he could claim he had some, god-given right to the land. Even if they didn't believe in it, as long as the people of the area did, it should hold some weight.

"Alright." Alexander nodded. "Might as well give it a shot. How difficult could it be to untie a knot anyway?"

Alexander nodded and shifted in his seat, getting comfortable and settling in for a long day of strategizing.

Very difficult, as it turned out. After several more weeks of travel and various stops at the villages and city-states along the way, they'd finally arrived in Gordium. Initially, they'd been met with distrust and hostility from the city guards but when Alexander had announced that he was here to try his hand at the knot, they'd relaxed a little. Of course, his army would need to camp outside the city, but he, Hephaestion, Cleitus, and Regulus had been allowed to enter and stay in the palace to try the knot as many times as they pleased.

Alexander had balked about the fact that there wasn't an attempt or time limit to the task and shrugged off all warnings that the knot was truly impossible to untie unless you were truly chosen by the gods. However, three days into the endeavor and Alexander was beginning to believe it.

Alexander lay on the ground in the chamber that contained the knot and stared at it, sitting on the floor next to him.

"How, in the name of the gods... did they tie this thing?" He was annoyed and exhausted, but mostly he was just impressed.

CHAPTER FOURTEEN

He glanced over to Hephaestion who was also laying on the marble floor, arm over his eyes. "I take back everything I said about this being a stupid way to determine leadership."

Hephaestion chuckled and flipped over onto his stomach so he was eye level with the knot as well. "In all my years of military work, I have never seen a knot like this one. The fact that this piece of rope has both of us stumped will haunt me until the day I die."

"How much longer are Cleitus and Regulus going to be in the library?" Alexander asked, poking the knot with his pointer finger.

"I don't know." Hephaestion replied. "They mentioned that they only got through half of the knot-making books yesterday so they will probably be there for a while."

Alexander flipped onto his back and groaned, rubbing his eyes with the heels of his palms. "I think I'm more stressed out than I was when we were fighting the battle on the river all those weeks ago."

Alexander heard Hephaestion move but didn't register what he was doing until he felt Hephaestion's hands on his thighs. Alexander opened his eyes and raised an eyebrow.

"Well." Hephaestion said shyly. "I don't think I can untie this knot for you, but I do believe that I can help with your stress."

Alexander felt himself twitch with interest. It had been almost a month since they'd been able to be intimate with each other. It was true that they slept in the same tent but every night after riding all day, winning over villages, or fighting small battles they were so exhausted that after the nightly strategy meeting with Regulus they both passed out almost immediately. "Is that so?" Alexander grinned. "How do you plan to do that?"

Hephaestion moved his attention to Alexander's pants and pulled them down exposing his groin. Hephaestion took Alexander in his hand and leaned down to lick at the tip. "I'm sure I can figure something out."

Alexander groaned as Hephaestion took him into his mouth and began to suck. Alexander had almost forgotten how incredible it felt to have Hephaestion in this way. He let the creases in his brow smoothen and let his head tilt back so it was resting on the marble floor. Hephaestion continued his minstrations, swirling his tongue around the head as Alexander hardened in his mouth. Alexander reached down and unable to reach Hephaestion's head, clenched his fists as his side instead.

Hephaestion took him all the way down to the hilt, his cock hitting the back of Hephaestion's throat and Alexander moaned as Hephaestion swallowed around him. Lazily he opened his eyes, he registered the room around him but a majority of his attention was on Hephaestion's hot mouth. His hips thrust up slightly in time with the bobs of Hephaestion's head.

"Ah...nghhh..." Alexander groaned, feeling himself building to orgasm. It had been such a long time that he was ready to burst. His breathing quickened and he knew that the noises coming out of his mouth, were warning to Hephaestion that he was close. The weapons hanging on the walls began to blur as he reached his peak; Alexander let out his voice, groaning, as he released into Hephaestion's mouth and throat, Hephaestion swallowing it all down.

Alexander relaxed his body as the last of his orgasm left him, he opened his eyes, the upside-down wall coming back into focus. "Mmm... you were right Hephaestion, I really just needed..." Alexander cut himself off as something on the wall came into crystal clear focus, Alexander sat up.

"What? You alright?" Hephaestion asked, the playful look on his face gone.

Alexander turned around and stared at the wall. "It couldn't be that simple."

"What couldn't be that simple?" Hephaestion mirrored his sentiment as they both got up off the floor, Alexander tucking himself back into his pants. Quickly he turned around and took Hephaestion's face in his hands.

"Were there any rules about how we untied the knot?" Alexander asked quickly, searching Hephaestion's face.

"No." Hephaestion shook his head slightly, following Alexander's gaze to the wall. "Why? What are you thinking?"

Alexander let go of Hephaestion and walked over to the sword mounted on the wall. Carefully he took it by the hilt and pulled it down, walking back over to where they had been sitting before. He leaned down and picked up the knot, holding it up to the sword and looking back at Hephaestion.

"What?" Hephaestion prompted, still not understanding what Alexander was suggesting.

Alexander adjusted his grip and found a place in the knot where the rope protruded slightly. Then, gently, he slipped the blade underneath the rope and pulled. The sword was sharp and so it only took minimal effort for the metal to cut through the rope. Alexander put the blade on the floor and began unraveling the knot until he was standing there mouth slightly open, staring at a length of rope, unknotted, in his hands.

He and Hephaestion stared at each other, then the rope, then back at each other. After several moments of silence, Hephaestion began to laugh.

"Did that moment of post orgasm clarity just give you the secret to becoming the ruler of Asia?"

Alexander regarded him for a moment before also bursting out into laughter. They were doubled over, clenching their sides and laughing when Cleitus and Regulus walked back in.

"We searched all the books but couldn't find... what's going on here?" Regulus inquired. He opened his mouth as if to say something else but his eyes locked on the rope in Alexander's hand and nothing came out.

"Well damn," Cleitus spoke, dropping the book he was holding onto the ground and walking over to pat Alexander heavily on the back. "All hail the new king of Asia, I guess."

Alexander was careful to put the sword back on the wall the way he'd found it before leaving the room with his group and presenting the rope to the priest who guarded the chamber. The priest stared at them with wide-eyed disbelief and quickly ran into the room to check that the knot was actually gone. When he confirmed that it was, he immediately fell to his knees and bowed. Alexander asked him to get back up and handed him the rope; that night his troops were allowed inside the walls. All of his men got a good night's sleep in the barracks and the horses got the care they deserved after so long on the road.

Their stocks were replenished and Alexander and his team were welcomed into the inner chambers of the palace and tended to like kings. That night Alexander and Hephaestion lay awake, still reeling in utter disbelief.

"You know that there will be people who still do not accept you as king because of this right?" Hephaestion whispered, laying next to Alexander in the giant palace bed. Alexander nodded, of course he knew that. They'd only just heard of the legend themselves recently.

"Yes, but it did allow us to take at least one city peacefully." Alexander pondered, playing Hephaestion's hair. Hephaestion made a soft noise of agreement.

"So, how far do you plan to extend this empire of yours?" Hephaestion asked into the dark room. "You've already expanded farther than your father ever did, won't you want to go home soon?"

Alexander thought about it, considering the pros and cons. Obviously, the further he expanded the empire, the more respect he would get as a commander and a leader and he was still pretty fresh from the betrayal at Thebes. Then again, he could always return home and work on policy, but he had Antipater in the capital for that. Antipater had been one of his father's closest advisors and he trusted him to care for the city in his absence. He wrinkled his nose as he thought of his mother, laying in wait for him to return, take a wife, and begin producing heirs. As long as he was out here, expanding the empire, that was one thing he wouldn't have to worry about.

"Perhaps until Olympia dies and I don't have to worry about her marrying me off to every eligible young woman who looks my way." Hephaestion snorted and interlaced his fingers with Alexander's. Alexander moved his head on the pillow until he was nose to nose with Hephaestion and he cupped the back of Hephaestion's neck lovingly.

"I love you," Alexander murmured into the darkness.

"I love you, too." Hephaestion's smile tugged at the corners of his mouth. "Alexander?"

"Hm?" Hephaestion covered the hand Alexander had on the back of his neck with his hand and rubbed it gently with his thumb.

"If you weren't king and you didn't have to worry about producing heirs, what kind of life do you think we could have?" Hephaestion's voice was steady but behind the calm demeanor, Alexander could hear the hesitation. Almost as if Hephaestion was worried Alexander would say that nothing would be different at all.

"If I weren't king," Alexander spoke as if he were thinking about it for the first time, though he'd thought about it many times before. "You and I would live together in a small estate in the country. Somewhere close enough to the city that we could make trips in every now and then for supplies and vacations, but far enough away that we wouldn't have to worry about the politics of the inner-city.

We'd have a garden where we could grow our fruits and vegetables, maybe some seasonal flowers and we'd tend chickens, a goat, and maybe some sheep. Perhaps Barsine could live on the estate and help with the household chores in exchange for a safe place to live away from her father's prying eyes.

In the mornings we would wake early, with the dawn and drink tea, taking some time to read or write together. We'd spend our days tending our garden and animals and maybe even pick up a hobby. In the evenings, we would dance together in the kitchen as dinner cooked and cuddle up next to the fire. Then, you'd take me to bed, make sweet love to me and we'd fall asleep side by side."

Hephaestion was quiet for a moment before Alexander heard him sniffle. Drawing back slightly Alexander saw a single tear falling from Hephaestion's eye.

"You've thought about it?" Hephaestion asked misty eyed.

"Of course I have," Alexander replied, wiping a tear from Hephaestion's cheek. "I meant it when I said I have no desire to marry any woman and that I love you."

Alexander paused and shrugged. "You're my best friend, and I don't know what I'd do without you."

Hephaestion pulled Alexander tight to his chest and kissed him on the lips. "Me too."

Alexander smiled and drifted slowly to sleep in Hephaestion's arms.

15

Chapter Fifteen

The resistance they'd expected despite their victory with the knot came a lot sooner than they'd hoped. After riding out from Gordium, it was not too long before one of his scouts came back to inform them that they had gained the attention of the Persian king Darius III, who was on his way to oppose them. Alexander expected this, he'd known that their peaceful expansion could only last so long. Smaller cities transferring their loyalty for protection was one thing but the larger cities and Persian nobility would not roll over easily.

On their way from Gordium to Issus, the army encountered a few stray Persian troops and had several small battles that took out a portion of Alexander's men, but nothing too impactful. Still however, he needed to drop off the sick and wounded in the city to be cared for before he led the rest of his men to the Syrian Gates where his scouts had informed them Darius would pass with his troops.

Issus was a nice city, full of plenty of people who had heard how Alexander conquered the Gordian knot, willing to tend to his men. The entire way to the Syrian Gates, Alexander discussed tactics and potential defensive positions they could take once they reached their destination, waiting for Darius to pass. The plan was to line the walls of the canyon with their archers and ready the cavalry behind a rock formation where they couldn't be easily seen. Alexander would stand in view of the upcoming army with his infantry and lure them in.

It was a great plan, which was why it was increasingly odd that they'd been in position for several hours now and their scouts sent in the direction Darius's army was supposed to be approaching from had not yet returned. Surely, if they'd been intercepted already, Darius's army would be upon them. The other option confused Alexander even further, they surely couldn't be so far away that it had taken this long for the scouts to reach them.

"Something's wrong," Alexander spoke, turning to Hephaestion and Regulus.

"I thought so too," Regulus said, walking up to stand next to Alexander. "So about an hour ago, I sent more scouts in the three other directions to see if they came upon anything, but nothing yet."

Then as if his words had fulfilled a prophecy, the men turned at the sound of hurried hoofbeats coming down the valley the way they'd came.

CHAPTER FIFTEEN   191

"General!" The scout was shouting, out of breath and panting. "The army... it's at Issus!"

"What?" Regulus demanded stopping the scout's horse.

"They passed another way and they have already made it to the city. They're..." The scout faltered.

"Out with it man," Regulus demanded.

"They're slaughtering our men."

Alexander felt the dread like a stone in his stomach. Suddenly he was brought back to that terrible moment at Thebes, when the soldier had burst into the tent to inform Alexander that part of his army had stormed the city and was raping and pillaging their way through the innocent civilians. He felt his head begin to spin, lost in his thoughts when he felt Hephaestion's firm hand grip his arm, grounding him. He snapped back and realized everyone was watching him, waiting for their next orders.

That was right, this was nothing like the situation in Thebes. This was just war and he was the commander, he needed to get them through this.

"Ready the troops and ride back to Issus immediately," Alexander commanded walking over to where his horse was waiting. Regulus intercepted him as he swung his leg up over his mount.

"Sire, if I may, we should ride back with haste but we need to be careful about reentering the city." Alexander watched him and stayed silent so he could continue. "I know you want to save as many of our men as possible, but..." Regulus tailed off.

"By the time we get there, they'll all likely already be dead." Alexander finished, letting the truth of what he'd said settle on him like a heaviness on his shoulders.

"Alright." Alexander regarded Regulus. "We will ride back but stop in the mountains across the river from the city so we can keep the higher ground while we figure out a plan."

Regulus saluted and Alexander began to ride, leading the troops back the way they'd come. Pretty soon, Hephaestion caught up and rode side by side with him, silently offering his support. Alexander took the ride to calm his breath and sort his thoughts. Hephaestion's presence was reassuring and helped him keep his mind on the task at hand; whenever he felt his mind wandering or falling down the rabbit hole of anxiety and doubt, he would just look to his right, and there he was, steadfast and strong.

When they finally crested the hill and looked down upon the city of Issus, it looked much as it had when they'd left it save the enormous army camped directly outside the gates. The city itself hadn't been a battleground as the only men they'd left were the sick and injured. It was a low blow to slaughter men already weakened by injury or disease, but Darius did not seem to care.

CHAPTER FIFTEEN   193

It reminded Alexander of how his father used to fight and it brought a bad taste to his mouth.

As if reading his mind, Hephaestion placed a hand on Alexander's shoulder. "Not everyone can be as kindhearted as you Alexander."

Alexander turned his head and covered Hephaestion's hand with his own. "I know."

Alexander gathered his generals to discuss the strategies he'd come up with on the ride over. While his father had been a ruthless fighter, his strengths lying in brute force and decimating the enemy, Alexander was a strategist. He'd always exceeded in outmaneuvering his opponents even in situations where the odds seemed unlikely.

"Parmenion." Alexander addressed one of his generals. "You take your troops and stick to the seaside, your job will be to block the Persian troops from moving around to flank us."

"I will lead the rest of the troops across the length of the Persian troops and we will surround them, backing them up against the city walls so they have nowhere to go."

His generals nodded in understanding as he laid out the routes by drawing them with a stick in the sand. It wasn't the best situation, but it could have been worse. Obviously, Alexander would have preferred to have more time to plan their attack, but now that Darius and his army had avoided their carefully laid out defenses at the gates and were already in the city, they had to do the best that they could with the situation at hand.

Alexander sat on his horse at the top of the hill, looking down upon the Persian army, his own men lining up in his peripheral vision. Taking a deep breath, he let the circumstances of the situation settle in his mind. Since his father had passed, Alexander felt the realities of being a king and ruling a kingdom hit him repeatedly. Just as one thing was resolved, it felt as though three other things popped up demanding his attention. Yet...

Alexander glanced to the side where Hephaestion sat on his horse, ready to ride down into the fray and fight alongside him. Knowing that Hephaestion was here with him let him sit taller in his saddle and lead the way he wanted.

As they rode down to meet the Persian army head-on, Alexander felt his confidence grow. The trust and confidence of the generals at his back was enough to inspire him to be the commander that they needed. The fight was brutal but in the end and against all odds, they actually won. This was a true turning point for Alexander as a king, boosting his confidence in himself, putting to rest all concerns any of his men may have had about his competence as a general, and finally earning him the respect that he craved so deeply. He could feel his father's shadow growing smaller and smaller the further they pushed on.

Through Tyre, Gaza, founding Alexandria, and defeating Darius at Persepolis, the ghost of Alexander's father became a distant memory. This was how he was meant to lead his people, expanding the empire with Hephaestion at his side. Years passed and Alexander grew accustomed to life on the road, he forgot all about needing to keep up a ruse that he was bedding women. He felt like he could breathe again. Life was simpler, and Alexander appreciated it for what it was; so when Alexander received the letter from Pella it was as though a rug had been pulled out from underneath him.

"Letter for you sire."

Alexander was reclining on the bed in his tent, Hephaestion napping peacefully next to him. Alexander extended his hand and waved the soldier off when he placed the parchment in Alexander's palm. Hephaestion stirred as Alexander broke the seal.

"Sorry love, did I wake you?" Alexander leaned back on one arm and kissed Hephaestion's forehead, running his fingers through his dark hair.

"Mmm." Hephaestion turned to face Alexander and pulled him down to kiss him gently on the lips. "It's alright. What's that?"

"Letter from Pella," Alexander replied nonchalantly, unfolding the parchment. "It's likely the quarterly report, or perhaps its another letter from my mother telling me how much she misses me." Hephaestion laughed softly, running his fingers up and down Alexander's thigh.

"Regardless, I'm sure it's n..." Alexander stopped mid-sentence, pausing to re-read the first paragraph, sure that he'd read it incorrectly.

Or misinterpreted it...

Or hallucinated...

Alexander blinked several times and rubbed his eyes, sitting up straighter and bringing the letter closer to his face.

"Alexander?" Hephaestion propped himself up on his elbow and ruffled his brow, looking concerned. "What is it?"

"I..." Alexander shook his head slightly. "I have to go back to Pella."

"What?" Hephaestion sat up fully now, the blanket falling off his chest and crumpling in his lap. He leaned in and read over Alexander's shoulder.

Your Highness,

CHAPTER FIFTEEN 197

We have recently received word from many of the nobles and they believe it is high time to take a wife. I have done my best to keep them at bay but with considerable interference from Olympia, they are now up in arms about it. Particularly with you leading the men into battles, there are questions about the line of succession and what should happen if you were to die. Olympia took it upon herself to reach out to Oxyartes who offered you marriage to his daughter, Roxana, years ago and accept on your behalf.

I tried to tell her that she did not have authority but she assured me that you wouldn't care who the woman was as long as it was a politically advantageous marriage. I am sorry Sire, I could not stop her.

Regardless, your presence is required back at Pella as soon as possible to sate the doubts and ease the concerns of the nobles and members of the court. We will await your arrival.

Yours,
Thetima

Alexander felt the paper crinkle in his hand as he tightened against it.

"Alexander," Hephaestion whispered, his arm winding around Alexander's waist.

"I..." Alexander felt a lump form in his throat. "I don't..."

Olympia took it upon herself to accept on your behalf.

Alexander thought his heart might beat out of his chest. There was no way that he could refuse, turning down Oxyartes's daughter at this point would be like spitting in the face of the nobleman. Besides, what was he going to do instead? Find another woman to marry? The very idea made him sick to his stomach.

He thought of Barsine, spending her days lounging in the place and coming to his aid when he requested her, only for them to drink wine and talk. He had known that would only buy him time, not act as a permanent solution, but he hadn't thought the time would come so soon. He thought of Hephaestion, holding him, kissing him, making love to him... to produce heirs, he would need to...

Alexander's breath picked up and he felt bile rise in his throat. He crumpled the letter in one hand and threw it across the room, burying his face in his hands. He needed to calm down, he needed to think, he needed... to figure a way out of this.

He had to.

Alexander felt Hephaestion's hands cup both sides of his face and turn his gaze.

"Alexander, breathe with me." Hephaestion cooed, rubbing his thumbs in small circles on Alexander's cheeks. "That's right... In... out... good."

"What if we just don't go?" Alexander asked weakly.

"Baby." Hephaestion's expression broke and he blinked as if holding back tears. "You know we can't do that. We knew this was coming, remember? We talked about this."

Alexander let Hephaestion pull him into his arms and lay them down. "I know but..." Alexander said lamely. "It feels different when it's actually happening. I feel like I can't breathe, like I can't escape."

"Shh... shh, I know." Hephaestion held Alexander tightly, and Alexander cried. He let himself feel the devastation of everything that was about to happen. He'd known that this was coming one day, but he'd thought he would be ready for it. In hindsight, he should have known better. No one can ever truly be ready to be forced into a life that they never wanted, no matter how much they believe they will be. In the end, he knew what was expected of him.

16

Chapter Sixteen

Alexander hadn't spoken a word since they crossed the boundary back into Pella. He didn't feel as though he could. Everything he tried to express dried up and died in his throat before ever seeing the light of day. The last five years, Alexander had worked incredibly hard to feel like the king everyone saw him as. He'd fought alongside his men, bested enemies on the field and in the negotiation rooms, and won the respect and trust of his troops. But riding back to the palace right now, he felt like that 20 year old kid, finding out that his father was murdered and lashing out in agony in the cells.

He couldn't raise his head past the horse's ears, he couldn't turn his gaze to look anyone in the eye, and he couldn't command anyone. Not like this.

His men had known something was wrong when he'd announced that he needed to head back to Pella and left Regulus in charge of the forces. He promised he would be back soon, but he was not sure if he could keep that promise and he knew it, his men knew it too. He'd grown quite close to the generals of his

CHAPTER SIXTEEN   201

army, spending long evenings chatting by the fire and drinking, telling stories and exchanging advice. He'd only confided in a couple of them that he was not interested in women but his relationship with Hephaestion was a well known fact among the men.

When he'd announced the reason for his departure, many of his men had been excited for him but he did see the pain in his generals' eyes, in the ones who truly understood what this meant.

As they approached the palace, Alexander saw an entourage of people waiting to welcome them back.

Great, he thought. Just what I needed.

Among them, he did see some familiar faces like Thetima and Barsine, but his blood turned cold when he saw Olympia, waiting in her exquisitely adorned robes, smiling as though she had done nothing wrong. They stopped at the palace doors and dismounted, handing the reins of their horses to the servants. Barsine ran up and gave him and Hephaestion hugs, whispering to Alexander how happy she was to see them alive and well. Thetima bowed her head but accepted Alexander's embrace when it came.

As Alexander continued up the stairs, he drew closer and closer to his mother. The smug look on her face confirmed everything he'd already known. She was pleased with herself for getting him back here and trapping him in a situation of her own design. Alexander grimaced and stepped to the side out of her reach when she moved to embrace him.

"Don't touch me Olympia." He growled, staring daggers.

"Oh Alexander, don't be that way." Olympia feigned hurt and tilted her head. "Come, give your mother a hug."

One of Alexander's generals stepped between them and suggested she move away. As she started to complain, Alexander turned to the palace guards. "I don't care what she does but I don't want her anywhere near me, do you understand?"

Olympia, who hadn't expected this, was speechless, eyes wide. Alexander turned to Thetima indicating that she walk with him.

"Is there any chance we can send a messenger to intercept them before they leave to make their way here?"

"Oh, Alexander." Thetima slowed their pace and touched her hand to his arm. "They're already here."

"Fuck." Alexander closed his eyes and rubbed the bridge of his nose. "Fuck!"

Hephaestion appeared next to them and Thetima quickly disseminated the same information. Alexander searched desperately for an answer, some sort of strategic move that he could make to sidestep this marriage that wouldn't cause an international incident to put his ability to rule in question. When he came up with nothing, he opened his eyes again, looking up at Hephaestion.

"I'm not getting out of this, am I?" Hephaestion said nothing but instead put a hand on Alexander's shoulder and squeezed. It said more than he could have out loud.

It's going to be okay. We will get through this together.

Alexander nodded in understanding and turned back to Thetima.

"Where are they?"

Thetima led them to a meeting room just off of the gardens; inside sat Oxyartes, his guard, and Roxana. She looked the same as he remembered if not a few years older. Her black hair was tied back away from her face and cascaded down her back and shoulders. She wore a traditional Bactrian gown with a veil that fell from the circlet on her head and the robes were a deep blue, an indication of their status.

"King Alexander." Oxyartes stood, welcoming them into the space, despite it being Alexander's palace. Alexander had to actively control his face so not to grimace.

"Oxyartes, Roxana, how good of you to come." Alexander got out, nodding to each of them as he spoke their names. Roxana looked up as he called her name, looking surprised that he would even address her at all.

"Well." Oxyartes continued, "When your mother informed us that you were ready to marry and form an alliance, we dropped everything and made our way over as soon as possible."

Alexander gave Oxyartes a tight lipped smile. "Yes, well... as soon as I heard you were on your way I rode back as quickly as I could."

Not technically a lie. Alexander walked over to the table and took his seat across from the Bactrian man, Hephaestion taking the seat next to him.

"I'm sure there are many things that need to be discussed." Alexander began, but was immediately corrected.

"Actually, your mother has taken care of most of the details already."

Of course, she had.

"Roxana's dowry arrived yesterday and Olympia was more than happy to help move everything to the treasury. We have been given lodgings and Roxana is ready to be moved into your chambers at your convenience." Oxyartes bowed his head, Roxana following suit.

This would have been great news had Alexander actually wanted to go through with this marriage. As it was, this was the worst thing that could have possibly happened. If he went back on this marriage now, it would cause irreparable damage to all parties involved. Alexander realized he hadn't said anything in an extended period of time when Hephaestion's hand came to rest on his thigh underneath the table.

"Yes." Alexander got out. "Excellent. I'm sure my mother has planned a date as well."

"Indeed she has." Oxyartes replied, raising his head. "The wedding is scheduled for the end of the week."

Alexander nodded, taking in the information presented to him. "Excellent. I'm sure you understand, I have been on the road for quite some time, so I will take my leave now." Alexander got up, the rest of the room standing with him.

"Of course." Oxyartes and his men bowed and Roxana dipped lowly in a curtsy.

Alexander nodded curtly and stalked out of the room, one purpose in mind. He turned the corner and addressed one of the guards.

"Bring me to my mother."

Olympia was sitting in her quarters, writing a letter when Alexander stormed in with his guards. Immediately the men got to work, taking away her writing utensils despite her protests and clearing the room of anything she could possibly use to communicate.

"Alexander." She exclaimed, in genuine upset. "What do you think you're doing?"

Alexander did not address her directly but instead turned to the guard he'd ordered to remain stationed in her room. "My mother is not to have any communication with the outside world, she is to remain in this room, and have meals brought to her throughout the day. She will be allowed to take escorted trips to the baths once a day and continue to enjoy her lavish accommodations."

"Alexander..." Olympia began but was immediately interrupted again.

"She will be allowed to attend the wedding so as not to cause embarrassment to the family but if she speaks she will immediately be brought back inside with no potential to rejoin the celebration. Aside from that, she will live, eat, exist here in this room until her heart gives out and she dies."

Alexander turned his attention to his mother, genuine hatred in his eyes. "You have crossed a line, not only as a mother but as a subject to a king. What you have done cannot be undone and you will bear the consequences of your actions for the rest of your life. Should you choose to make trouble or fight against this decree, I guarantee I can make your stay considerably less comfortable."

Olympia, for once in her life, said nothing. Alexander wasn't sure if it was shock that prevented her from speaking or if it was her self perseverance telling her not to argue, but he didn't care. Alexander turned on his heel and stormed out of the room, guards closing and locking the doors behind him.

When Alexander got back to his room, Hephaestion and Barsine were there, sitting on the bed talking.

"Oh, Alex." Barsine cooed sympathetically as he entered. "Hephaestion told me everything."

Alexander allowed himself to be pulled down onto the bed and into Barsine's embrace, his cheek resting on her pillowy breasts. He wrapped his arms around her waist and let her comb her fingers through his hair. Hephaestion rubbed circles in his back and kissed his shoulder comfortingly.

"You don't have to let her move in, you know." Barsine spoke up finally. "You will likely have to spend the night with her after your wedding but after that, she can keep her own quarters. You won't have to live with her, you'll just have to..."

"Have sex with her." Alexander finished. "I have to produce an heir."

"Yeah." Barsine sighed. "If it's any consolation, I know how you feel."

Alexander allowed himself a small sound of amusement.

"If I had to have sex with either of you I think I'd be pretty upset too."

"Gee, thanks." Hephaestion chided playfully.

"No offense." Barsine shrugged.

Alexander sat back up and ran his fingers through his hair, Barsine and Hephaestion watching him carefully.

"Well. I suppose there's nothing we can do to stop it now." Alexander felt each word stab through him like a blade. It truly was out of his control, despite being king and having all the power in the world, he was still powerless to prevent this.

17

CHAPTER SEVENTEEN

The wedding was full of excitement and joyous celebration and Alexander tried his best to fake it. He did his part, dancing, eating, drinking, and marrying Roxana. He kissed her during the ceremony and she was soft, delicate, and all wrong; to get through it, he pictured Hephaestion but when he leaned back and caught his gaze from across the room, Hephaestion looked as pained as Alexander felt.

The festivities died down after midnight and Alexander brought Roxana back to his chambers as he was expected to. He'd done well faking it all night, but when the doors closed behind them he found himself adrift, without an anchor or any idea of what to do. He took a deep breath and turned around only to find Roxana standing in a pile of her robes, the veil still draped over her face.

Alexander started so badly that he bumped into the dresser, sending a vase crashing to the floor. Immediately he averted his eyes, desperately searching for something, anything to say.

"Are you alright, Sire?" Roxana asked, sounding genuinely concerned.

"Yes... yes. I'm fine. I'm - sorry..." Alexander stuttered, forcing himself to make eye contact with her. "And we are married now, I think you can call me Alexander." He tried, extending an olive branch.

"Yes si... Alexander. Whatever pleases you." Alexander didn't think he'd ever felt so uncomfortable in his life. "Would you like me to come to you? Or..." Roxana trailed off and he realized that he was still pressed up against the dresser on the opposite side of the room.

"Oh... no. I, uh, I will come to you." Alexander swallowed, closing the distance between them as best he could without shaking or running in the opposite direction. He stepped gingerly, his eyes moving everywhere except her naked body. He'd seen naked women before, he'd just never seen one in this context. There were... expectations. Ones he wasn't sure he could meet, and that terrified him.

He lifted the veil off of her face and placed the circlet on the bedside table. She really was beautiful, Alexander mused, he truly wished that things could just be easier. Roxana searched his eyes for a moment, her gaze dropping to his crotch and clearly flaccid dick, before dropping to her knees.

"Wh... what are you doing?" Alexander asked dumbly.

CHAPTER SEVENTEEN 211

Roxana smiled up at him softly. "Helping you get in the mood." Alexander inhaled sharply as she ran her hand up his thigh and over his cock. Hephaestion did this for him all the time, but it did not feel good right now, in fact, it made him a little nauseous.

He couldn't look at her, so instead he directed his gaze upwards, to the ceiling. He felt her pull his pants down and take him in her hand, giving a few cursory strokes.

Nothing.

You have to do this. Alexander thought. *Come on, just pretend it's Hephaestion.*

Alexander closed his eyes and pictured Hephaestion on his knees; his hot breath replacing Roxana's, the way that he would run his hands up and down Alexander's thighs. He pictured Hephaestion stroking himself as he serviced Alexander and he felt his cock twitch slightly.

There we go. Come on.

Hephaestion's eyes, his mouth, his cock, his sexy body...

Roxana's lips found the inside of his thigh and Alexander tensed up. This wasn't Hephaestion, he could tell, and suddenly the images of Hephaestion twisted into memories of that night in Troy when Hephaestion thought he'd slept with Barsine. The tears running down his cheeks, the hurt in his face, the way he'd physically recoiled when Alexander had reached out.

"Stop." Alexander heard himself say and Roxana stopped moving instantly. Alexander opened his eyes and looked down at her, meeting her beautiful gaze. She looked confused, and Alexander felt terrible. "Let's... let's not do this tonight..."

Roxana's expression was searching as she watched Alexander tuck himself back into his pants and help her stand.

"Is something wrong si... Alexander?" Alexander took a deep breath and shook his head.

"No, I'm just tired." He was aware that this was a weak excuse and he knew that she knew it too, but he was eternally grateful that she asked no questions. Instead, she climbed into the bed and slid between the sheets silently. Alexander walked over to the lamps and snuffed them out, climbing into bed next to her.

He did not reach out to her, did not pull her close, and did not do any of the things he knew he was expected to do on his wedding night. After a few minutes he heard her breathing even out and he glanced to the side. She was turned away from him, facing the wall. Alexander did not know if she was genuinely asleep or if she was faking it, but either way he was grateful. He rubbed his eyes and turned onto his side, facing the other direction and told himself that he would sleep and deal with it in the morning, but in his heart of hearts, he knew there would be no sleep for him tonight.

CHAPTER SEVENTEEN

When the morning came, Alexander waited until the sun crested above the mountains and shone into his window before getting up and sneaking into the bathroom to bathe. He got the feeling that she would not follow him, but just in case he made it quick, only pausing to rinse once he was done. He'd brought his clothing in with him to dress in a separate space and once he was clothed, he meandered sheepishly back into the room to find Roxana, up, dressed, and sitting at the windowsill.

"Good morning." Alexander tried. Roxana turned her head and smiled sweetly. "How did you sleep?" Alexander could see the circles under her eyes and guessed that she'd slept about as well as he did.

"Very well, thank you." Roxana replied.

Okay, so she wasn't going to bring up his refusal of her last night. Alexander shifted and took a breath.

"We should go, they will have breakfast waiting." Roxana stood and bowed her head slightly in acknowledgment.

They walked together in silence to the main hall and sat side by side as the servants brought food. Of course Olympia was nowhere to be seen since she had been confined to her quarters, but his guard, Barsine, and Hephaestion were there. Barsine kept glancing over at Hephaestion who looked worse than Alexander did, his eyes were puffy and he was barely eating anything, instead opting to push his food around his plate.

Breakfast was silent and uncomfortable, nobody outside of the primary group was really sure why but no one said anything. As everyone was wrapping up, Barsine spoke, breaking the silence.

"Your highness, ma'am." She said addressing Roxana. Roxana looked up in surprise at Barsine. "Would you do me the honor of allowing me to show you around the gardens this morning?"

Roxana raised her eyebrows and glanced at Alexander, who was paying zero attention, but instead mirroring Hephaestion and pushing food around on his plate.

"I..." Roxana started. "I would love to."

Barsine stood and walked over to their side of the table, leaning down to whisper in Alexander's ear. "Talk to him."

Alexander came back to himself understanding what Barsine was doing. As she passed, he caught her hand, exchanging a silent thank you before letting her go and watching the two women walk out together. Alexander stood and gestured for Hephaestion to follow him, Hephaestion got up slowly and walked after Alexander out of the main hall and into the library. The door shut and Alexander turned to face Hephaestion, who looked like he was on the verge of tears.

"I couldn't do it." Alexander choked out. He watched several expressions pass over Hephaestion's face; relief, sadness, concern, and finally understanding. Hephaestion opened his arms and Alexander threw himself into them. "She tried to... and I tried to let her... I thought of you... but..."

Hephaestion pet Alexander's head, holding him close. "Alexander..."

"I'm sorry." Alexander pulled back and met Hephaestion's gaze. "I know I should have, but I couldn't. I kept thinking about how upset you'd been when you thought I'd slept with Barsine and..."

"I know." Hephaestion murmured, pressing kisses into his hair. They stood that way for quite some time before Hephaestion took him by his shoulders and squared them, looking at Alexander from his arm's length. "Okay." Hephaestion said, with finality.

"Okay?" Alexander asked, watching Hephaestion's face turn from despair to resolve.

"You just have to get her pregnant." Hephaestion nodded resolutely. "I was in my head driving myself crazy all night thinking about you making love to someone else. But, now that I see that you couldn't even let her touch you that way, I just want to get this out of the way, for both of us."

Alexander opened and closed his mouth a couple of times, not understanding what Hephaestion was saying.

"Look." Hephaestion continued. "Don't kiss her, don't make love to her, just fuck her. Get yourself to the very edge and then put it inside her, just get her pregnant. Then we can be done with all of this."

Alexander thought about it and found himself nodding his head. "Okay, I think I can... maybe that would work."

Hephaestion took his face in his hands and pressed their foreheads together. "You will only ever make love to me, but you need an heir. It's okay."

Alexander bit his lip and nodded. This might work...

"Okay." Hephaestion nodded, catching his gaze one more time before reaching behind him and locking the door. Hephaestion kissed Alexander with all the passion and fire that had been lacking last night with Roxana. As their tongues collided, Alexander felt himself stir immediately, his cock coming to life. Hephaestion pressed their hips together and Alexander wrapped his arms up under Hephaestion's arms and over his shoulders from behind.

"But first." Hephaestion whispered, biting at Alexander's lip. "I want you to fuck me."

"What?" Alexander pulled back slightly to see Hephaestion blushing slightly.

"I know we haven't before, but I've been thinking about it for a while and I want to be your first. That's part of why I was so upset last night." Alexander's gaze softened and he kissed down Hephaestion's jaw and neck.

"Are you sure?" Alexander asked, biting at Hephaestion's ear.

"Yes." Hephaestion said resolutely, moving Alexander's hand to his ass. Alexander squeezed experimentally and felt Hephaestion's hips shift forward, his hardening length pressing into Alexander's hip. Alexander kissed Hephaestion, backing them up to the couch that sat against the side wall. As they reclined together, Hephaestion's hand worked its way down between Alexander's legs and began rubbing his length.

Alexander moaned softly, rocking his hips in time with Hephaestion's strokes. "I want you to open me up, Alexander." Hephaestion licked Alexander's ear and gave his cock a squeeze before turning over, presenting his ass to Alexander.

Alexander swallowed, they'd never done it this way before, but Hephaestion had made love to him so many times that he knew how it was supposed to go. He pulled Hephaestion's pants down and bit into the swell of his ass; he stuck one finger in his mouth, lubing it up and circled it around Hephaestion's entrance. "You ready?" Alexander asked, pressing the pad of his finger against the tight ring of muscle.

Hephaestion responded by pushing his hips back onto Alexander's finger, the digit sinking into him. They both groaned, Alexander as he felt Hephaestion clenching around him at the sudden intrusion. As Hephaestion had done for him so many times before, Alexander began pumping his finger in and out, rotating it to search for that pleasure spot that he knew was there.

He needed to get deeper, so he inserted a second finger, grabbing Hephaestion's hip as he scissored his fingers, pressing deeper. He flipped his wrist, positioning the pads of his fingers upwards and pulled slightly with his middle finger at he deepest point. When Hephaestion moaned loudly, clenching down on him, he knew he'd found it.

"You like that?" Alexander teased.

"Holy shit... is that what it's like for you all the time?" Hephaestion asked breathlessly.

"Pretty much." Alexander grinned and kept pumping his fingers in and out, brushing up against Hephaestion's sensitive spot with each pulse.

"I've been... hnggg... missing out, clearly." Hephaestion laughed through the throes of pleasure. Alexander smiled to himself and added a third finger, however it wasn't very long before Hephaestion was rocking his hips back into Alexander and mewling desperately.

CHAPTER SEVENTEEN   219

"Please..." Hephaestion begged. "Fuck me... I need you."

Alexander felt a surge of arousal shoot through his body at Hephaestion's words. He pulled his fingers out and shifted onto his knees, lining up his throbbing cock with Hephaestion's ass. Slowly he pushed himself inside and as soon as he was halfway in, he almost came right then and there.

"Fuck," Alexander groaned. "You're so fucking tight- it feels so good..." Hephaestion moaned loudly again as Alexander pushed even deeper. Once he was fully sheathed inside him, Alexander paused, getting accustomed to the feeling and pulling himself back down from the edge. He wanted this to last.

"Alexander... move, please..." Hephaestion moaned, pushing his hips back even further, connecting Alexander's hips to his ass. Alexander pulled out experimentally and thrust back in, pulling a pleasured moan from both of them. He took hold of Hephaestion's hips and began to rock at a more rhythmic pace. When he finally got the hang of it, he tilted his hips slightly changing the angle and thrusting in harder.

Hephaestion threw his head back in a silent cry as Alexander slammed into him. Alexander made love to Hephaestion with everything he had, pistoning his hips until he could feel himself one breath away from the edge.

"Hephaestion... Fuck, I'm gonna cum." Alexander panted out, but before he could say anything more, Hephaestion cried out, his insides clenching around Alexander so tightly he couldn't have held back his orgasm if he tried. Hephaestion shot his load onto the couch, untouched, and Alexander's eyes rolled back in his head as he came inside, filling him up.

When the final waves of orgasm rolled through them, Alexander leaned down and kissed Hephaestion before pulling out and shifting so Hephaestion could snuggle down into his lap.

"That was incredible." Alexander whispered, holding Hephaestion close. "I'm so glad it was you."

Hephaestion hugged him tighter and buried his face in Alexander's neck. "One day it will be able to be just us, I promise."

CHAPTER EIGHTEEN

Alexander steeled himself, standing outside the door to his bedroom. He'd requested Roxana's presence again in his bed and waited until he knew she was already inside to come out of hiding and head back to his quarters. He and Hephaestion had talked about it at length while they laid on the couch cuddling and had come up with a few strategies to make it happen.

It should have been weird, talking like this with Hephaestion but oddly enough, it made him feel better. His guilt had stemmed from the fact that he'd never wanted to see Hephaestion upset the way he had been in Troy; he didn't want to betray him. However, now it felt more like this was a situation they could suffer through together. Hephaestion knew everything that was going to happen in his bedroom and encouraged it; whatever made it happen so they never had to do it again was fine with him.

Alexander took a deep breath and opened the doors. Roxana was sitting on the bed in her nightgown, watching him with careful eyes.

"Hello." Alexander said sheepishly. Roxana bit her lip nervously and smiled the best she could.

"Hello."

Alexander closed the door behind him and walked over to the bed, sitting down across from her. "I'm sorry about last night." He began, this part was easy because it was true. He really was sorry, Roxana was such a kind, lovely woman, she deserved much better. "Truly, I was just exhausted."

Roxana searched his face as if she knew he wasn't being entirely honest but said nothing.

"If it's alright with you, I'd really like to try again." Alexander peeked up at her, meeting her gaze. There was something mildly distrustful in it but she smiled and bowed her head.

"Of course Alexander."

Alexander let out a breath he didn't know he was holding and nodded. "Alright, where do you want me?"

Roxana lifted her eyebrows but moved off the bed, migrating over to where Alexander was sitting, and settling between his legs. "Here is fine." Alexander nodded and swallowed trying to remember what Hephaestion had told him.

A mouth is a mouth, it will feel mostly the same. Just close your eyes and imagine it's me doing it.

Alexander pulled his pants down and let her take him into her hand. Alexander closed his eyes and focused on creating the image he and Hephaestion had talked about. Alexander's breath hitched slightly as a tongue flicked a couple of kitten licks against the tip of his still flaccid cock. It did feel good, so far things were going according to plans so he leaned back slightly onto his palms and let her continue.

Upon seeing that he was not going to push her away as he had last night, Roxana took him into her mouth. It was warm and Hephaestion was right, it felt mostly the same. His eyes were still screwed shut but in his mind, Hephaestion was the one kneeling between his legs, hard and enthusiastically sucking his cock. He felt himself harden slightly, considering that a win.

He was beginning to feel his breath pick up slightly, leaning heavily into the fantasy when he felt a small, feminine hand on his thigh. His eyes flew open, the fantasy shattering; he tried to let her continue but almost immediately his erection went away and Roxana stopped, looking up at him in confusion.

"Um." Alexander fumbled for something to say. "I must still be tired. We can try this again tomorrow."

Alexander stared at the headboard, too ashamed to look his wife in the face. He knew it was a terrible excuse, but he didn't have anything else he could say. He set his jaw resolutely, they would try again tomorrow and this time he would be more prepared. He heard Roxana get up and leave, but could not bear to turn his head away from the wall until he heard a familiar voice.

"Alexander?" Alexander turned his gaze towards Barsine's voice. He felt tears of embarrassment burning in his eyes but met her gaze nevertheless. Her face softened and she came over to sit down with him, her hand slipping into his. "Didn't go well?"

"I..." Alexander looked down at his lap. "No."

Barsine took a deep breath and pulled Alexander in for a hug.

"What are you doing here?" Alexander asked, "How did you know?"

"Hephaestion had to leave the grounds on business tonight and told me to watch over you. He explained everything."

Alexander sighed in relief, grateful that he didn't have to explain, sinking further into Barsine's embrace.

The next couple of nights went mostly the same; Alexander would summon Roxana to his chambers, they would start being intimate and something would happen causing Alexander to fall out of the fantasy. A sound, a touch, her hair, each night it was something new and Alexander became increasingly frustrated with himself. By the end of the week, he even waited to summon her until he was already fully aroused and just tried mounting her from behind as he had Hephaestion, but immediately went soft.

That was probably the worst one. By the next week, Alexander was so full of shame and self-hatred, he was glad Hephaestion wasn't here to see him fail so miserably. So when Alexander arrived in his chambers that night, Roxana was nowhere to be found. He stood confused for a moment until movement in the hallway caught his attention. He turned to see Barsine approaching, a confused look on her face.

"Barsine, where is Roxana?" Alexander asked, glancing behind her to see if she had accompanied her tonight. Barsine pursed her lips and crossed her arms over her chest.

"You mean, you didn't send for me?" Alexander blinked a couple of times in confusion and shook his head.

"No, who told you that?"

"Roxana." Barsine huffed, sounding irritate. "I went to fetch her for you and when I arrived at her room she would not come with me. She said that you had requested me instead tonight."

Alexander felt embarrassment and frustration boiling in his blood. "What the fuck." He spat. Immediately he set off down the hallway towards Roxana's chambers. Here he was, putting in all this effort, just for her to decide that she didn't want to deal with him not being able to get it up tonight?

Typically, Alexander would never barge into another person's chambers unannounced but he was just so overcome with anger that when he arrived at her doors, he did not bother to knock, just bursting in. Roxana looked up from her bed in surprise as Alexander slammed the door shut.

"Why did you lie?" Alexander demanded. Roxana avoided his gaze and he stomped over to the side of her bed to look her in the eyes. "Why did you tell Barsine that I called for her instead of you?"

"I thought you would be pleased." Roxana responded icily.

"Why the fuck would I be pleased?" Alexander asked exasperatedly, incurring a confused look from Roxana's face.

"Well... because..."

"Here I am, trying desperately to produce an heir like my kingdom demands of me and for some reason, my wife is uninterested."

Roxana set her jaw and frowned, "I am hardly uninterested."

"What then?" Alexander demanded. "Get tired of your husband's incompetence in bed? Thought you'd just pass the terrible burden to someone else?"

"Of course not." Roxana said defensively, "It's just clear to me that you do not want to have sex with me, so I thought that

I could give you a break from trying to force yourself to do something you don't want to do." Her voice raised slightly and she sat forward on the bed.

Alexander felt his cheeks burn. "I don't need a break!" Alexander shouted. "I need to produce an heir."

"Well, I don't know how to help you with that when you clearly find me so horribly repulsive!" Roxana yelled back and Alexander recoiled as though he'd been slapped. "You can't seem to stand me for enough time to enjoy a simple blowjob, let alone produce an heir. I'm sorry that you find me so unattractive and I'm sorry that I'm not enough but I can only take so much rejection before I need to send in someone you actually want to fuck!"

Alexander laughed incredulously. "So why the fuck did you send Barsine? Huh? I've never fucked her either!"

Alexander's anger immediately fled from his body as the words left his mouth. He swallowed, feeling the blood drain from his face.

"What?" Roxana stopped in her tracks, staring at Alexander.

"I..." Alexander stuttered, unsure of how to continue. The only people who knew that Barsine was not Alexander's actual lover were Alexander, Hephaestion, and Barsine and now he'd just gone and told his largest secret to someone he barely knew.

"She's your concubine. What do you mean you've never slept with her?" Alexander searched Roxana's face for some sort of ill-intent but all he found was the face of a lovely woman who'd gotten her hopes up and been rejected so many times that she'd resorted to locking herself in her room.

"Fuck." Alexander mumbled, rubbing his eyes and sitting down on the bed. He'd been so preoccupied with his own feelings on the matter that he'd never stopped to consider how Roxana was feeling. "I'm a terrible person."

Roxana had leaned back slightly and was warily watching him from the side of her eye. Alexander sighed and turned to face her.

"You are my wife." He started, reaching out for her hand. She almost pulled back but didn't in the last second, letting Alexander take her hand in his. "I owe you the truth, at least."

"I hope you won't tell anyone, but I will understand if you have me because of how I've treated you." Alexander took a deep breath. "I like men... exclusively men."

Roxana watched him, the wheels turning in her head.

"Hephaestion and I have been together since I turned 18 and I've never... with a woman... he's the only person I've ever been with."

Roxana furrowed her brows and pursed her lips deep in thought. "But Barsine?"

Alexander nodded. "We've never been like that. I met her at that party in Troy some years ago and her father was trying to force her to marry. She didn't like men in that way and everyone around me was pressuring me to either take a wife or find a lover. Other than Hephaestion, she's my best friend and I do love her, but not that way."

As the final piece of the puzzle fell into place, Roxana looked back up at Alexander, tears in her eyes. "Oh god. I was so horrible to you." She placed her hand over her mouth. "I just thought... I know that Bactrian beauty standards are different from Macedonian ones and I thought you thought I was..."

"Oh, no." Alexander leaned forward and took Roxana's face in his hands, wiping the stray tears from her cheeks as they fell. "Roxana, you are absolutely beautiful, it's not your fault you aren't him. I'm sorry if you ever felt like I was disappointed or upset with you, I was angry at myself for being unable to perform my duties."

"Alexander..." Roxana breathed.

"After all this, I really do hope that we can be friends. Though, I will understand if you never want to see me again. You will have your own quarters and will not be bothered. I don't want you to worry about your father or ever being without a place to stay, I vowed to take care of you and I will keep my promise."

Roxana's gaze softened and she cupped Alexander's face in her hand. "How did I get so lucky to have such a kind and attentive husband?" She smiled softly and Alexander let out a breath.

"So..." He tried. "You won't tell?"

Roxana shook her head. "I won't tell and don't worry about the situation about an heir. We will figure it out together, okay?"

Alexander blinked back tears at Roxana's promise. Never before had he considered anyone a life partner except Hephaestion, but despite knowing that he could never love her the way she wanted, Roxana was still willing to stand by his side. It was a different type of partnership for sure, but a partnership nonetheless and Alexander was eternally grateful to have it.

19

Chapter Nineteen

Hephaestion returned later that night and in that time, Alexander had gotten the chance to know Roxana better. She enjoyed music, walks in the garden, and after clearing things up, became close friends with Barsine. Barsine was thrilled to have another person around who knew the truth that she could talk to in confidence when the boys were away. Barsine explained to Roxana the logistics of pretending to fuck the king and Roxana, being the intelligent woman she was, caught on quickly.

Barsine and Roxana took turns "bedding" Alexander and sometimes they'd even show up together. Those nights were often the most fun as Roxana and Barsine would play off each other until they had collapsed into a fit of laughter being stifled by their hands or pillows.

One night, as Barsine slept, Alexander and Roxana laid awake next to each other. Alexander had grown much more comfortable sleeping next to Roxana now that she knew the truth, in fact, they had become fast friends once Alexander had come clean.

"So." Roxana ventured, turning onto her side to look at Alexander. Alexander turned to face her as well. "You and Hephaestion are leaving for India soon, is that right?"

"That's the plan." Alexander replied noncommittally. Truthfully, Alexander wasn't looking forward to leaving, he understood that it was his duty to continue expanding the empire but he'd grown rather fond of their arrangement and little family. Roxana pursed her lips and a look fell across her face. "What?"

As if Roxana hadn't realized she was making a face, she shook her head and smiled. "Nothing. I will just miss you, that's all."

Alexander smiled and caressed her cheek gently. "Don't worry." Alexander reassured her. "We will be back faster than you will be able to get bored without us."

Roxana smiled and rested her palm on top of Alexander's hand. Quickly, they both fell asleep, tired and comfortable.

Alexander was reclining on his bed later that week when Hephaestion entered unannounced. This wasn't odd considering that they often slept together when Barsine and Roxana were not occupying the spaces in his bed. What was odd, however, was Roxana tagging along behind him. Alexander raised an eyebrow as she closed the door behind her.

"Your wife, is a genius." Hephaestion announced, grinning. Alexander glanced over to Roxana who was just blushing and doing her best not to look away in embarrassment.

"Well, I knew that." Alexander responded, shutting his book. "But what is the reason for this sudden revelation?"

Hephaestion took Roxana by the hand and pulled her over to the bed, sitting them both down. "She has figured out a solution to the 'heir' problem."

Alexander raised both of his eyebrows in surprise and looked back and forth between the pair, waiting for someone to explain. "Is that so?"

"Yes." Hephaestion smiled shyly. "You can't get it up when it's just her. So, what if I was there too?"

"Uh." Alexander said dumbly, not quite understanding where this was going.

"Roxana." Hephaestion deferred, gesturing to her. "Explain."

"Well." Roxana was flushing as if she felt like she shouldn't be talking about this, but continued anyway. "You have no trouble having sex with Hephaestion, so I was thinking, you two could... you know and at the very end before you... well..." Roxana dodged back and forth between Hephaestion and Alexander, waiting for his reaction.

Alexander opened his mouth to respond but nothing came out. His immediate reaction was to say, no that's a terrible idea. But in truth, it might just work. Had she suggested this early on when they hadn't known each other well, he would have turned her down flat out. However, she knew that he and Hephaestion were together so he wouldn't have to worry about her finding out how deeply in love with him he was. Alexander shut his mouth again and considered it.

"You know." He stated. "That might work, actually."

Hephaestion's grin spread and Roxana's eyes grew wider in surprise. "Really?"

"I told you." Hephaestion threw his arm around Roxana. "So, when is the best time to do this?"

Roxana flushed deeper but replied. "Well, I am actually in the time right now where the midwives tell me I will be at my most fertile."

The three of them let the words drop and settle between them. Hephaestion nodded and scooted closer to Alexander. "Well, there's no time like the present then, is there?"

Alexander turned to meet Hephaestion's gaze and found himself inches away from Hephaestion's lips.

"If anyone gets uncomfortable," Hephaestion prefaced. "Say something and everything will stop. Okay?"

"Okay." Alexander agreed. Together they looked over at Roxana who seemed confused why they were checking in with her.

"I mean, it was my idea, so…" Roxana trailed off but Hephaestion and Alexander each grabbed one of her hands.

"We know that." Alexander replied.

"But," Hephaestion exchanged glances with Alexander before turning his attention back to Roxana. "You're not just a means to an end Roxana, you're our partner too and we won't move forward with this unless you're okay with it too."

Roxana blinked rapidly, tears accumulating at the corners of her eyes. "You guys…" Alexander squeezed her hand and offered a smile. Roxana considered for a moment before nodding. "Yes, okay."

"Alright." Hephaestion rose off the bed to turn down the lights, leaving only a few oil lamps on bathing the room in a warm, sensual light. Hephaestion climbed back onto the bed and glanced at Roxana for final approval before leaning in and pressing his lips to Alexander's.

Alexander sighed into the kiss, winding his fingers into Hephaestion's hair. He opened his mouth, letting Hephaestion lick into it, their tongues tangling familiarly. Hephaestion ran his hands down each side of Alexander's torso, sending shivers down Alexander's spine. Hephaestion moved forward, laying Alexander down on the bed and climbing on top of him. As they kissed, Alexander was aware of Roxana watching but did not feel put off by it.

Hephaestion lowered his hips to meet Alexander's and they both groaned as Hephaestion rolled his hips gently over Alexander's. Alexander felt his length hardening beneath his lover and he ground his hips up slightly, seeking relief. Alexander let a moan escape his lips as he felt Hephaestion's growing erection brush up against his own and he grabbed onto Hephaestion's shoulders for better purchase.

He let his kisses travel down Hephaestion's jaw and to his neck where he kissed, bit, and sucked on his pulse the way he knew Hephaestion liked. Hephaestion growled and reached down between them moving their clothes out of the way and wrapping a hand around both of their lengths. Alexander let his head fall back as Hephaestion stroked them and kissed at Alexander's collarbone.

"It's been a while since you've taken my cock." Hephaestion whispered teasingly in his ear. "Are you sure you're ready for it?"

"Yes." Alexander responded a little too quickly. "Yes, please." Hephaestion grinned devilishly and pulled Alexander's pants completely off, exposing him. Hephaestion placed a single digit into his mouth and dragged it out slowly and sensually, teasing

Alexander before reaching down between his legs and pressing his finger inside him. Alexander keened, cock bouncing against his stomach as he tilted his hips slightly to further accommodate the intrusion.

Hephaestion continued to use his fingers to open Alexander up and Alexander turned his attention to Roxana on the end of the bed. Her face was flushed and she watched them with heavy lids, her hand disappearing underneath her robe. Alexander's eyes rolled back as Hephaestion added a second and third finger, curling them to rub against Alexander's sensitive bundle of nerves.

Alexander felt precum leak from his cock and onto his abs as Hephaestion rubbed mercilessly. He heard Hephaestion speak as he helped him up, not fully registering his words. Turning him around, Hephaestion kissed down Alexander's neck and shoulder as he lined himself up. Alexander whimpered, pressing back against Hephaestion's cock, desperate for it.

Hephaestion was breathing heavily, mouthing at Alexander's pulse as he pressed inside. Alexander sighed in relief, his insides accommodating Hephaestion, fitting him snugly and perfectly. Hephaestion began thrusting shortly at first to create a rhythm before gesturing for Roxana to come over. Alexander was so hard and blissed out that he barely registered Roxana on her elbows and knees in front of him until he was sinking into her heat.

She felt different than Hephaestion had and he was sure that had they been alone, this would have been a moment where he would have fought to stay aroused. However with Hephaestion inside him from behind, grabbing at his body and thrusting into him, Alexander's cock remained hard and leaking.

Hephaestion placed one arm around Alexander's shoulders and the other at his hips, starting to thrust again rhythmically. Alexander couldn't help it, his hips rocked back to meet Hephaestion's thrusts but at the same time, his cock burned with pleasure as Roxana clenched around him. It was like the drag created when Hephaestion would jerk him off while making love to him but so much warmer, and wetter. Hephaestion didn't give him much time to think about it, instead holding him tighter and pounding into him harder.

Alexander moaned loudly, one of his hands finding Roxana's hip and the other winding up into Hephaestion's hair. Hephaestion tilted his hips slightly and Alexander cried out as Hephaestion rammed directly into his sensitive spot.

"Fuck." Alexander shivered. He felt so full and achingly hard that he could barely register what was going on around him. As Hephaestion continued to thrust into him, Alexander felt a familiar heat building in his stomach, being expedited by the pressure on his cock.

"I'm..." He stuttered. "I'm gonna cum... fuck."

"Yes, yeah... cum for me baby." Hephaestion murmured sensually in his ear. When Hephaestion licked up the length of his ear and nibbled softly on his earlobe, Alexander felt himself spill over. His hips stuttered as he came, filling up Roxana with his seed. Hephaestion cursed as Alexander clenched around him, and he thrust forward one final time, groaning loudly as he also fell over the edge.

The three of them collapsed onto the bed, laying naked on the sheets. Hephaestion and Alexander held each other, showering the other with kisses as Roxana migrated to the top of the bed, putting her feet up on the wall and laying on her back.

"Holy shit." Alexander laughed breathlessly. "It worked."

Roxana started giggling next, triggering Hephaestion to start laughing too. Alexander was vaguely aware of the door opening and closing as someone snuck in. He turned his head to see Barsine looking between all three of them expectantly.

"Well?" She asked, a smile spreading across her lips. Roxana tilted her head back so she could see Barsine.

"Ta da!" She held her arms out on the bed as if she'd just completed a trick. Barsine laughed and ran over to the bed, joining them, kissing Alexander and Hephaestion on the forehead and cheek respectively and placed Roxana's head in her lap, stroking her hair.

Alexander smiled to himself and relaxed into Hephaestion's arms, thanking the gods that there were so many people who loved and cared about him.

20

CHAPTER TWENTY

The next few weeks were a blur, preparations for the campaign to India had begun and Alexander was busier than he'd ever been. Barsine stayed with Roxana in her chambers for the next few days to ensure she stayed in bed and continued to rest, promoting the best chance for pregnancy. The week they were supposed to leave, Hephaestion was scarce and Alexander just chalked it all up to preparations being stressful.

However, as they were about to leave, Alexander turned the corner to see Hephaestion deep in conversation with Roxana and Barsine. He looked incredibly distressed and even more so when Barsine slipped him something that he stared at for quite some time before putting into his pocket. Alexander moved slightly closer so that he could hear what they were saying.

"Are you sure this is the only way?" Hephaestion bit his lip the way he did when he was nervous. Barsine nodded.

"You know that if he knew, he would try and stop you." Alexander frowned, they were keeping something from him. He felt a pang of pain in his chest; he knew Barsine and Roxana probably had their secrets that they kept from him but Hephaestion? He thought they shared everything.

Before he could determine anything more, the sound of guards echoed down the sound of guards echoed down the hallway and the group dispersed. Alexander took a deep breath and turned the corner.

"Hephaestion." He called and Hephaestion turned, several emotions flashing across his face before he could mask them with his typical smile. He clearly hadn't expected to see Alexander so soon after the conversation with Roxana and Barsine. "Are you ready to go?"

Hephaestion smiled softly and walked over to meet Alexander. "Yes. Are you?"

"I am." Alexander eyed Hephaestion suspiciously. "Is everything alright?"

Hephaestion turned, seemingly startled by the question. "Yes, of course. Why?"

Alexander pursed his lips and debated telling Hephaestion what he'd seen but decided against it. "You've just seemed distant this week." He lied.

Hephaestion smiled and cupped Alexander's face in his hands, kissing him softly. "I'm fine. I promise."

"Alright." Alexander replied skeptically, a sadness blossoming in his chest.

The several weeks of campaign went by quickly, the mysterious conversation all but forgotten as Alexander and Hephaestion fell back into their typical rhythm being on the road. They had finally arrived at the Hydaspes River and fought a grueling battle against King Porus, the king of the Eastern Indian kingdom. Alexander founded two separate cities, one on each side of the river and was on his way back to his tent to celebrate when he saw Hephaestion reading a letter, just outside.

He looked absolutely distressed.

"Hephaestion?" Alexander called out, walking over to him. Hephaestion looked up and hid the letter behind his back. Immediately Alexander was flashed back to the secret meeting in the halls before they'd left and a wave of anger and hurt surged through him. "What is that?"

"Nothing." Hephaestion replied, turning to escape the tent. Alexander followed him and watched in horror as Hephaestion held the letter up to a candle flame and let it burn away.

"What are you doing?" Alexander demanded.

"It's nothing, Alexander. Please don't worry about it." Alexander shut his mouth and felt his face heat up. Hephaestion's face looked both incredibly guilty and worried.

"It's clearly something." Alexander replied exasperatedly. "Does it have to do with the secret meeting you had with Barsine and Roxana before we left?"

Hephaestion's mouth fell open at that and he searched Alexander's face for more information. "You knew about that?"

"I stumbled upon you as we were preparing to leave." Alexander said sourly.

"How much did you hear?" Hephaestion's face was white now.

"Just that you were doing something that I couldn't know about." Alexander spat. "I thought we didn't keep secrets from each other Hephaestion." Alexander's voice broke and he felt the tears accumulating at the corners of his eyes.

Hephaestion's expression changed into one of understanding. "Baby." He closed the distance between them and trapped Alexander in a bruising hug. "I love you so much, and I need you to know that everything I do, I do for you. Okay?"

Now Alexander was confused. What could he possibly be doing that Alexander couldn't know about?

Alexander took Hephaestion by the shoulders and stared at him. "Hephaestion, what's wrong? Are you in trouble? Please tell me! I can help."

Hephaestion just shook his head and cupped Alexander's cheeks in his hands pressing a kiss to Alexander's lips. "I need…" Hephaestion started but pulled back and looked Alexander directly in the eyes. "I need you to trust us, okay?"

Alexander opened his mouth to protest but something in Hephaestion's gaze stopped him and he just nodded. Hephaestion pulled back and placed one more kiss on Alexander's forehead. "Get some sleep okay? I will see you later, I have to take care of something."

Alexander watched as Hephaestion left the tent, the pressure of his lips still tingling on his forehead.

I need you to trust us, okay?

Alexander set his jaw, they'd never lied to him before. Hephaestion was right, he just needed to trust them. Alexander slept fitfully that night, unknowingly getting some of the last sleep he would get for quite some time before he woke to a fresh hell in the morning.

When Alexander woke up, he was not alone. Regulus stood in his tent, lips tight, calling his name.

"Your Highness." Alexander's eyes shot open and he instinctively reached to the side for Hephaestion, but he wasn't there. Alexander swallowed remembering their conversation from the night before.

"Yes Regulus? What is it?" Alexander replied sleepily.

"It's Hephaestion." That immediately got Alexander's attention.

"What? What's wrong?" Alexander practically jumped out of bed, throwing on his clothes. "Take me to him."

Regulus wouldn't meet his eyes but led Alexander outside and in the direction of the medical tent. "He came by the med tent late last night, saying that he wasn't feeling well and…"

"Is he alright?" Alexander demanded, speeding his pace.

"The doctor assured me that he would be fine and that there was no need to wake you."

"Regulus." Alexander prodded, sounding about as panicked as he felt.

"Well, he took a turn in the night…"

"No." Alexander felt his heart drop into his stomach and he broke into a run. When he arrived at the medical tent, he threw open the flaps and nearly threw up. There, laying on the cot was

Hephaestion, looking pale and sickly; but that wasn't the part that nearly killed him.

Hephaestion wasn't breathing.

"No. No, no, no, no, no, no!" Alexander chanted, rushing over to the cot and dropping to his knees, taking Hephaestion's face in his hands.

He was cold.

"Baby, baby, no... please... no." Alexander sobbed, burying his face in Hephaestion's chest, desperate to hear a heartbeat. Desperate to feel him breathe, to have his hands in his hair again, to kiss him again. Alexander shook violently, holding him; he had never felt this depth of despair ever in his entire life and he knew in his heart that he never would again.

Images flashed in his memory; Hephaestion kissing him for the first time, telling him that he loved him, all those times he slept in Hephaestion's arms...

"He can't be gone." Alexander demanded through tears. "He can't!"

The doctor placed a single hand on Alexander's shoulder, which he shoved off. "I'm sorry sire, he is. We are going to cremate the body for transport back to the city where a funeral can be held."

"You shut up." Alexander bit back. "You shut the fuck up." He tried to stand, collapsing back down onto the ground, his anger breaking back into sorrow. "Hephaestion... Hephaestion... Baby... please... wake up."

Alexander sobbed, holding Hephaestion's hand tight to his lips. "I can't..." Alexander's voice broke. "I can't do this without you."

But Hephaestion didn't respond. He didn't run his fingers through Alexander's hair, he didn't squeeze Alexander's hand back, he didn't... do anything. Alexander gripped his chest as his heart threatened to rip apart. "Please." Alexander pleased one last time. "I love you."

Alexander wasn't sure how long he sat there, but he did have a vague memory of someone lifting him off the ground and bringing him back to his tent. The trip came in flashes, riding in a carriage, stopping to rest, staring at the sky blankly. He didn't even register when they returned to Pella, he felt the warmth of Barsine and Roxana embracing him but couldn't return it. He led the funeral parade somehow, finding himself back in his room before he could remember crying again.

He didn't eat, he didn't drink, he didn't sleep. He only lay in his bed, speaking to no one.

One night, he didn't know how much time had passed, Barsine visited him. He felt the bed dip under her weight but made no move to acknowledge her presence, he couldn't. She helped him sit up and tried to offer him a cup of tea, but he couldn't accept it, he couldn't even meet her gaze.

"Please Alexander." He heard her say as she placed the cup to his lips. "I just need you to trust us, okay?"

I just need you to trust us, okay?

Alexander's gaze rose to meet hers at the familiar words. For some reason, those words broke through his sorrow-addled haze and he nodded softly, allowing her to feed him the tea.

"All of this will be over soon, I promise." Barsine whispered to him as she helped him lay back down, then for the first time in however long it had been since that first night, Alexander closed his eyes and let the darkness take him.

21

Chapter Twenty-One

"Did you hear? The king is dead." The women whispered in the market.

"Really? How did it happen?" Another asked.

"He got sick I guess. Likely the same sickness that killed Hephaestion."

"That was such a shame." Another woman piped up and none of them acknowledged the man in the cloak walking through the market, down the cobblestone road, and out of town.

Winter was just beginning to melt into spring and the man stepped carefully, ensuring he wouldn't slip on a patch of ice as he made his way down the road. He paused briefly to open the gate when he arrived at the farm, slipping inside and petting the dog that came to greet him.

He walked inside, throwing off his cloak and hanging it on a hook by the door. He slipped off his shoes and walked over to the kitchen, placing the food he'd gotten at the market on the counter and beginning to prepare it. He smiled softly when he felt another pair of arms wrap around him and familiar lips, kiss his cheek.

"I heard some interesting news at the market today." The man kept cutting the vegetables as he spoke.

"Is that so?" The other man replied, burying his face in the crook of his neck.

"Evidently. The king is dead." He stopped chopping to grin to himself and turn around in the other man's embrace.

"Ah, word travels quickly doesn't it?" Hephaestion said in an amused tone as Alexander threw his arms around Hephaestion's neck.

"It certainly does." Alexander smiled and leaned forward, kissing Hephaestion and feeling Hephaestion wind his fingers into Alexander's hair, holding him close.

Alexander had woken up confused and drowsy in a cottage he didn't recognize after that night Barsine had visited him.

"Careful, don't try sitting up too quickly." Alexander's haze cleared immediately when he heard the familiar voice.

"Baby?" His head snapped to the side to see Hephaestion, alive and smiling at him, stroking his hair.

"Yes love, it's me." Hephaestion's voice cracked as tears streamed down his cheeks. Alexander ignored the doctor's protests as he scrambled to the edge of the bed and wrapped Hephaestion in his arms as tightly as he could, kissing him over and over again.

"You..." Alexander sobbed. "You were dead... I saw you..."

"No baby, I'm not, I'm here. I promise, I'm never going to leave you again." Hephaestion squeezed him back.

"See?" Another familiar voice penetrated the silence. "I told you it would work."

Alexander looked up to see Roxana and Barsine standing by the doctor, watching misty eyed. Alexander had sat, listening to their explanation of what had happened in great detail. Hephaestion had shared with Roxana one night his and Alexander's dream to escape the expectations and just be together. That's when the plan had been born.

Barsine had worked for months with the doctor, who Alexander now recognized as the man from the medical tent the night he'd thought Hephaestion had died, on a draught that would simulate death but not actually cause it. It wasn't without risk, of course, which is why they opted not to tell Alexander beforehand. That and as terrible as it had been, the public had to believe that Alexander was in such depths of despair that he could have fallen ill and died, no questions asked.

The draught that Barsine had given to Alexander that night had been a similar concoction to that they'd given to Hephaestion. It had been less potent because they only needed the doctor to declare Alexander as dead, not present him to anyone else. After declared dead, they'd worked with Regulus to move him out of the city, cremating another body in his place.

The entire time Alexander listened, Hephaestion did not let go for one second. He rubbed Alexander's back, kissed his face and neck, and held him. Once Roxana and Barsine had finished explaining everything, they gave Hephaestion and Alexander a moment alone. Hephaestion had apologized over and over again for deceiving Alexander but Alexander forgave him instantly, resolving never to let him out of his sight ever again.

They hugged, kissed, cried, and eventually fell asleep; leaving the rest of the logistics for the next day.

"Barsine came by while you were out." Hephaestion noted, grabbing an apple from the bag and biting into it.

"Is that so?" Alexander raised his eyebrows, smiling and turning back to the vegetables. "What is the news?"

"The council finally made a decision about the regency and Roxana was appointed yesterday."

"That's great news." Alexander replied, popping a piece of carrot into his mouth. "And how's the baby?"

"Healthy and growing." Hephaestion grinned proudly. "Roxana is complaining about her ankles hurting but other than that, it seems to be a pretty easy pregnancy."

Alexander smiled and put down the knife turning back to run his fingers through Hephaestion's hair. "I am the luckiest man on the planet." He proclaimed, pressing a kiss to Hephaestion's lips.

"That would be incredibly unlikely." Hephaestion teased.

"Oh really, why is that?" Alexander laughed as Hephaestion wrapped his arms around his waist, bringing them flush together.

"Because." Hephaestion said matter-of-factly. "I'm the luckiest man in the world."

Alexander smiled and let Hephaestion pull him into another, deeper kiss. "I love you so much." Alexander squeezed Hephaestion, pulling him in as close as he could.

"I love you too." Hephaestion said with a smile in his voice. "For the rest of our lives."

BOOKS BY HARLOWE SAVAGE

The Monarchs of Eros Series

Alexander
Emperor Ai
Hadrian

About Author

Harlowe Savage is a queer author dedicated to creating stories that depict queer romances with the same amount of spice and passion that readers get from their straight counterparts. She firmly believes that the gap between the amount of LGBTQIA+ erotica and heterosexual erotica in the mainstream is far too large and intends to rectify this through normalizing queer romance novels and increasing accessibility of the genre.

www.harlowesavage.com

instagram.com/harlowesavage/

tiktok.com/@harlowesavage

Made in the USA
Coppell, TX
29 January 2026

70325380R00152